The Case at Castle Rock Cove

Beau Monde Secrets, Book 4

Anne Rollins

ARE YOU SIGNED UP FOR DRAGONBLADE'S BLOG?

You'll get the latest news and information on exclusive giveaways, exclusive excerpts, coming releases, sales, free books, cover reveals and more.

Check out our complete list of authors, too!

No spam, no junk. That's a promise!

Sign Up Here

www.dragonbladepublishing.com

Dearest Reader;

Thank you for your support of a small press. At Dragonblade Publishing, we strive to bring you the highest quality Historical Romance from some of the best authors in the business. Without your support, there is no 'us', so we sincerely hope you adore these stories and find some new favorite authors along the way.

Happy Reading!

CEO, Dragonblade Publishing

Additional Dragonblade books by
Author Anne Rollins

Beau Monde Secrets Series
Secrets at Selwyn Castle (Book 1)
Discovery at Dogwood Cottage (Book 2)
The Incident at Ingleton (Book 3)
The Case at Castle Rock Cove (Book 4)

Chapter One

April 1822

CATO FOUND THE bottle first. He'd started the walk on a lead, but after a few minutes on the beach, he slipped his collar to run ahead. Ben ought to have been prepared for that trick. It was hardly the first time Cato had done it. He always chafed at the slow pace Ben set while searching the beach at low tide.

"Cato! Come here!" Ben called, though he knew Cato too well to expect him to return on command. Cato was an obedient dog when nothing distracted him, but it didn't take much to sidetrack him.

The brown-and-white dog acknowledged Ben's call with a wag of his tail but kept furiously digging in the damp sand. He had found the first potential treasure of the day, and he wasn't about to abandon it.

"That better not be something poisonous!" Ben broke into a slow jog, hurrying to cross the yards of damp sand separating him from his dog.

Like many dogs, Cato was willing to taste anything that looked and smelled even remotely edible. If the object buried in the sand happened to be a rotting fish, the potential for disaster was high. Even if Cato didn't ingest it and make himself sick to his stomach, odds were, he'd roll in it and need a bath. Dread of that chore sent Ben from a jog to a real run.

But by the time Ben reached the hole in the sand, Cato had

already moved on in search of new discoveries. *Not something edible*, Ben concluded. When he peered into the sandy hole the dog left behind, he found nothing but a green glass bottle.

At least it won't bite me. The last time Cato found something interesting, the something interesting had been a crab that attacked Ben.

He picked the bottle up carefully, but it appeared to be unbroken, with no sharp edges to cut him. The cork stopper had been coated in wax, presumably to keep out water. Inside the bottle was a roll of paper.

Ben's heart sped up. *The classic message in a bottle!* He'd never found one before. He turned the bottle around in his hand, wondering how long it had been in the water and where it had come from. Sand clung to the glass, but no chips or scratches marred the smooth surface. The cork also looked to be in surprisingly good condition, with no visible crumbling.

The bottle was not, therefore, a relic from a previous century, or even a previous decade, Ben concluded. He doubted it had traveled very far before being washed up on the beach below Castle Rock Point. Should he just throw it back into the water? Or leave it in the sand to become someone else's treasure?

He peered into his collection basket. All he'd found so far was a pretty shell, which he'd placed in the straw-lined right compartment of the basket. He had half a dozen shells just as pretty back in his workroom; there was really nothing special about this one.

When he first began combing the beach at Castle Rock Cove, he picked up everything that looked remotely interesting, from pretty rocks and unusual shells to bits of colorful sea glass. He'd brought it all into his bedchamber and spread it on a piece of oilcloth on the floor to dry out.

The housekeeper, Mrs. Smith, protested over the mess and the smell. Ben's aunt had taken one look at Ben's collection and sided with Mrs. Smith. She wanted Ben to throw the whole collection into the dustbin. As a compromise, Ben's grandfather assigned him a room above the carriage house and forbade him to bring his beach finds into the house.

Moreover, Grandfather Marlowe insisted that Ben must keep no more than one of his finds per day. "You don't need dozens of snail shells," he had said. "And you should leave some for other people, anyway."

"What other people?" Ben had protested. "Do you think fishermen have time to comb the beach for geodes?" Not that he'd found any geodes, mind you. But the principle mattered.

"There will be holiday sea-goers in summer," Grandfather Marlowe warned. "And they'll all want souvenirs. Don't hoard them all. You don't have room for all of them, anyway."

On days when he found nothing worth keeping, Ben had no trouble following his grandfather's rule. Other days, he was so torn between two different treasures that he had to make the decision by flipping a coin. Today, though, the decision was easy. He didn't have a bottle like this, and certainly not one with a message in it.

He tucked the bottle carefully into a cloth-lined compartment of his basket. Then he gently placed the rejected seashell in the pit Cato had dug. That would make a little mystery for whoever next walked along the beach.

Satisfied with the day's find, Ben called for Cato. This time, Cato galloped right up to Ben, his tongue hanging out of his mouth. A few energetic wags of his tail scattered sand every-where, including on Ben's Wellington boots.

"Atta boy!" Ben rubbed Cato's ears, then refastened the collar more tightly around the dog's neck. "Time to go home." Cato's tail slowed its enthusiastic wagging, but he followed Ben without protest.

There were two ways up to the cliffs above the cove: a rough path formed by years of use on the western side of Castle Rock Cove, and a man-made staircase cut into the stone on the eastern side. The staircase led straight up to Marlowe land. Technically, most of the cove belonged to the Marlowe estate as well, but

Grandfather Marlowe had never minded trespassers on the beach or the rocks that gave the cove its name.

Ben usually took the stairs; the other path made him nervous. The rocky earth along the western path had a habit of slipping alarmingly beneath his feet, and he found it hard to keep his balance on some sections of the zig-zagging trail. The stairs felt much firmer and more stable, though he still wished there were a handrail.

The lack of a handrail bothered Cato not a whit. He hadn't had a long enough run to wear him out, and he would have galloped exuberantly up the stairs if Ben had let him. But Ben kept them at a slow, steady pace until they reached the green field above the cliff. Then he broke into a run, making one small dog very happy.

Marlowe Tower loomed over the park. It had been built well back from the cliff so its owners wouldn't have to worry about erosion undermining the foundations—at least not for a few centuries.

From the front, the house looked like a genuine castle, with narrow windows for protection from a siege. Visitors approaching it for the first time usually thought they were visiting an ancient stronghold of the Marlowe family.

In fact, the tower was a sham. Elias Marlowe had built the house a mere fifty years ago. Inspired by the rise of Gothic fiction, he wanted a Gothic castle of his own. After acquiring a fortune through speculating, he bought the land from a dissolute nobleman, tore down the already-crumbling country manor, and had a faux castle of his own built in its place.

Elias did not live to see the castle completed, but his son, Joseph, brought his bride home to Marlowe Tower, and raised three daughters there. Two of the daughters married and flew the nest, but Faith Marlowe stayed behind. After an apoplexy carried Mrs. Joseph Marlowe away, Faith managed the house and served as hostess on the rare occasions when Mr. Marlowe entertained guests.

So far as Ben could tell, his aunt and grandfather had lived quite happily together. But when Ben decided not to finish his degree at Cambridge, his mother suggested he move in with his grandfather.

"They could use the company," Lady Radcliffe insisted. "Your grandfather needs someone more lively to cheer him up."

Ben had doubts about his ability to cheer anyone up, given how miserable he had been at Cambridge after his friend Baynton had died. Still, he listened to his mother, packed his trunk of clothes and a crate full of books, and moved to Dorsetshire.

Moving to Castle Rock Cove turned out to be one of the best decisions Ben had ever made. He not only enjoyed the quiet solitude of the tower but also loved having a beach full of treasure right at his feet. And his grandfather, rather than telling Ben to throw his whole messy collection out—as Ben's parents had done in the past—simply asked him to keep it out of everyone's way.

Today, Ben headed straight for his specimen room, taking the curving path that led around the side of the house and past the row of storm-blasted trees that formed a barrier between the house and the stables.

When he reached the carriage house, he let Cato loose from his leash. The dog hurried to his kennel in search of a leftover bone. Meanwhile, Ben entered the carriage house and pounded up the staircase, taking the steps two at a time.

The upper story contained only one room, and it was all Ben's. He closed the door, locking it behind him. It wasn't as if he thought anyone would try to steal his treasures—he knew most of them were valuable only to himself. But he did not like being interrupted while he concentrated on an interesting artifact, and he found the green glass bottle very interesting.

Ben wavered for a moment. He did not normally alter the objects he found on the beach, apart from cleaning them. Part of him would have liked to keep the bottle exactly as he found it: corked and sealed. But another part of him desperately wanted to know what was written on the letter inside.

His curiosity and his desire to collect warred for a moment. Curiosity won. He could not bear not knowing what the note said! He set caution aside to break the wax seal and draw out the cork. Coaxing out the scroll of paper was harder than he expected. In the end, he had to use a pair of tweezers to pull it through the neck of the bottle. Ben unfolded the paper with shaking hands, then paused to silently laugh at himself. How foolish it was to act as if this note was magical or life changing! As if it were a map to treasure or an appeal to rescue! Even if it had been tossed overboard by a sailor on a sinking boat, there was no way the sailor would still be alive, waiting for rescue.

But he could not ignore the frisson of excitement that crept down his spine when he unfolded the note and read it. At first the contents made his eyes widen; then they made him grin.

April 13, 1822

To Whomever Finds this Note:

Dear Sir or Madam, please rescue me! I am in dire peril of boredom. We are visiting my elderly cousin in Newell-on-Sea, and she does not own a single book worth reading. Her husband was a clergyman, and most of his books are collections of sermons. The closest thing to a novel is Pilgrim's Progress. *I have already read* Pilgrim's Progress *twice, though I have only been here a week! When I asked about a circulating library, my cousin told me there was no library of any kind in Newell. How can a seaside town not have a library?*

My mother, my sister, and I came here to convalesce after a bad case of influenza. The problem is that I am already recovered and in fine fettle, whereas my sister and my mother are recovering more slowly. They are not able to take long walks with me. They only want to bathe in the sea and rest. I hate bathing in the ocean, and I have already rested enough, thank you! I need something else to keep me entertained, or I will go mad from sitting inside all day.

I am going to stand on Castle Rock Point and hurl this bot-

tle into the water below the cliff. If you find this note months or years after I dropped it, all I ask is that you think well of me. And maybe, if there is still no circulating library in Newell, you should consider starting one.

But if you find this note before the end of June, 1822, then I beg you to rescue me from the tedium of this holiday. We did not bring our saddle horses, so I cannot ride, and even if I had a horse, there would be no one to ride with me. And, as I believe I have already indicated, I was unprepared for the lack of reading material.

Dear stranger, I beg your assistance! If, by chance, you find this note before our visit ends, I would be much obliged if you informed me of the direction of the nearest circulating library or bookshop. You can put your response in a bottle or jar on Castle Rock Point. Please do not throw the bottle into the ocean. If you do that, I will never find it. I never walk on the beach if I can avoid it.

If you are able to provide me even a moment of entertainment, I will forever be your most grateful and obedient servant,

W. S.

Ben's hands fairly trembled with eagerness. He would have been no good at rescuing a drowning sailor or resuscitating a child pulled breathless from the cold waves, but this? *This* was a problem he could solve! He had books enough for half-a-dozen convalescents. He had a saddle horse of his own, as well as a spare hack that his grandfather used to ride. That horse was elderly, yes, but still sound.

This W.S. sounded like a schoolboy, or perhaps a student only a little younger than Ben. But whatever W.S.'s age, Ben could undoubtedly be of assistance keeping him entertained. Best of all, there would be no awkward face-to-face introductions if they corresponded by letter. Ben was far better at communicating in writing than in speech.

Ben reached for the portable writing desk he kept on his worktable. First, he popped a lemon drop into his mouth. He kept a little crock of them in the carriage house, just as he did in his bedchamber, so he would always have one at hand when he buckled down to work. Then he drew out a piece of stationery, sharpened a quill with his penknife, and prepared to answer the letter.

Chapter Two

"WILLA!" MISS HADFIELD had fallen so far behind, she had to raise her voice. "We really had better turn back now! It is too cold."

Willa bit her lip and ducked her head, pretending she hadn't heard. Miss Hadfield was right, of course. It was a cold and cloudy day, and the wind drove at an angle calculated to cut through even a warm cloak. Worse, Willa thought she smelled rain in the air. It was hard to tell for certain, though, given the pervasive odor of the ocean.

How she *hated* that scent. It would forever remind her of those miserable years in Blackpool. It was half the reason she had objected to spending the spring at Newell. She'd argued intensely in favor of taking a cottage in the Lake District, which was much closer to home, anyway.

But the family doctor insisted that Phoebe and Mama would benefit from the ocean air, and Cousin Sarah had eagerly offered her own home, just off Newell's High Street. Mama had been happy to stay with a relative rather than taking lodgings in a resort closer to home. Now they were settled in and everyone seemed happy.

Everyone except for Willa, who wanted to pack a valise and run away. In London, the Season would be in full swing. Willa should have been trying on clothes at her modiste's and brushing up on her dance steps. Instead, she spent her days staring out the window, hoping someone interesting would walk by. If not a person, maybe a stray dog or cat?

By now, she'd reached Castle Rock Point. The view of the sea was undoubtedly impressive, but Willa hardly spared a glance at it. Instead, she scanned the space before the edge of the cliff. There wasn't much to see: thick grass, an iron bench placed so that holiday trippers could sit down and admire the view of the cove, and—there! A glint of glass!

Willa darted forward and grabbed the bottle. Whoever had found it had reused the original green bottle, corking it tightly. She tucked the bottle into the pocket of her pelisse and turned back to Miss Hadfield.

"We can go home now," she said brightly.

Miss Hadfield shook her head. The walk had turned her cheeks red, making her round face resemble a blushing apple. At least her hair remained confined in a tidy knot, unlike Willa's wild locks.

"I believe I'd like to sit down and catch my breath," Miss Hadfield said. If she noticed the way Willa's pocket bulged, she made no comment.

No one noticed the bottle when Willa and Miss Hadfield returned home, thoroughly chilled and ready for a hot cup of tea. As soon as she was out of sight, Willa hid the bottle in the trunk at the foot of her bed. She did not want to answer all the questions she'd be asked if anyone caught her uncorking it to remove the note inside.

Between one thing and another, Willa did not have the chance to read the letter until bedtime. As always, Phoebe was sent up to bed an hour before Willa. Usually, Willa would have stayed in the parlor with her mother, talking and stitching and trying not to look annoyed if Cousin Sarah told the same stories she had told yesterday.

Tonight, though, she feigned exhaustion and took a candle upstairs not long after Phoebe retired for the night. Luck was with her for once, Phoebe had fallen asleep quickly. Willa could read her letter without interruption or interrogation.

Willa unrolled the scroll of paper and eagerly scanned the reply.

Dear W.S.:

You do sound miserable! Perhaps I may be of service? I live above the cove, not much more than a mile from the town. If you have any questions about Newell or Market Caseton, you have only to ask. I mention Market Caseton because that is where you will find the nearest circulating library. Mrs. Thatcher runs a stationery shop, but she also sells periodicals and maintains the circulating library. The collection may seem sparse if you are used to London bookshops, but you will at least find something other than Pilgrim's Progress.

If all else fails, I can loan you some of my books. My personal library mostly consists of books of information, but I do have some novels and tales that may be of interest. Have you read Frankenstein, *or* The Vampyre? *Or, if you wish for something longer, I have a few of the Waverly novels. Only a few, though; historical novels are not quite my cup of tea.*

If you would like to ride with me, I could loan you a hack, as long as you do not ride more than 12 or 13 stone. I should warn you that I do not ride very far, though—mostly just about my grandfather's estate or down to the village. But there are some pleasant rides along the cliffs, and I should be happy to show you.

Of course, you may not desire company. There is nothing wrong with that, either. I often prefer solitude myself. If you like, I can leave a package of books for you at the bakery in Newell. People frequently trust Mrs. Plummer with passing along a parcel. I am afraid I cannot leave a mount for you that way, though! (I assure you, the bakery is too small for a horse.) I suppose we will have to meet in person if you wish to ride with me.

Please write back to inform me how you wish to proceed!
Sincerely,
B.R.

Willa grinned at the note in her hand. The prospect of making a local friend had brightened up the whole day. Maybe even the whole week.

She only wished B.R. had said more about herself. Was it too much to hope that B.R. might be close to Willa in age? She could not be a very old lady, or she would not still be riding a horse, Willa reasoned. Nor did she write like a busy matron trying to rear a half-dozen children. She might well be a spinster, though. Not that there would be anything wrong with that.

But Willa foolishly hoped that B.R. was an unattached young lady, someone who could chat about bonnets and books and the latest *on-dit* from the London papers. What, though, could the B. in the initials stand for? Beatrice? Betsey? Boudicia? Willa smothered a giggle at the last idea.

Since the hour was late, she could not reply to the note tonight. But the first spare moment she got tomorrow, she would answer it. She knew just the place to meet B.R.

The next morning, she had so much trouble finding time to respond that she kept her answer practical and short.

Dear B.R.,

I would love to borrow some of your books! But I would also like to talk with you about them. I have read Frankenstein, *but not* The Vampyre. *Even your books of information would be more interesting than my uncle's books of sermons.*

Will you attend church at St. Clement's this Sunday? If so, I could meet you in the churchyard after the service. I will be wearing a red cloak. If you are able to meet, simply leave a note for me at Mrs. Plummer's bakeshop. I may not be able to walk back to the Point again before Sunday.

If there is no note, I will assume that you are unable to meet, or that you had rather not have company. As you say, there is nothing wrong with solitude. But sometimes reading quietly with a congenial companion can be more comfortable than reading alone. The silence is not so loud then, if that be not an Irish bull.

In any case, I hope to hear from you again. But I do hope that we are able to meet after this Sunday's service!

Sincerely,

W.S.

This time, she did not seal the bottle with wax. It did not need to be waterproofed if she was going to leave it on dry land. She planned to hide it underneath the wrought iron bench, which might offer a little protection from the elements. If nothing else, it would make the bottle harder to see. Willa did not want a stranger to intercept her letter.

But getting the bottle out to the point proved more challenging than Willa had anticipated. There was no possibility of taking a walk that day. Rain began falling late in the morning, and it did not stop until dusk.

Willa suggested a walk the next day, but no one wanted to accompany her. Mama's lingering cough had worsened overnight, and she kept to her bed. Miss Hadfield insisted that after so much rain, the ground would be too muddy for a walk, and they must wait for it to dry.

The day after that, the ground was still damp, but Willa persuaded one of the maids to accompany her on a walk. If Maggie saw Willa leave the bottle beneath the iron bench, she kept all questions to herself, for which Willa was grateful.

Fortunately, the bakery was open every day but Sunday. On Friday, Willa convinced Miss Hadfield to let her stop there for tea cakes. It did not take much convincing, since Miss Hadfield was nearly as fond of sweets as Willa herself.

While Miss Hadfield and Phoebe picked out treats to take back home, Willa leaned forward and whispered to the matronly looking woman behind the counter. "Are there by chance any notes or packages from B.R. to W.S.?"

"Oh, are you W.S., then, dearie?" The woman smiled at her. "Yes indeed, there's a note for you."

She turned around and rummaged in a drawer. It took a

surprising amount of time for her to find the sealed letter, but find it she did, and she handed it to Willa.

Unfortunately, this time, Phoebe saw Willa take the letter. "What's that?"

Willa's heart skipped a beat. *Found out!* Then she reasoned with herself. What did it matter if anyone saw her accept a note? Wasn't she allowed to have friends?

The voice of her better angel whispered that she ought not have any friends who had not been properly introduced or of whom her mother might not approve. But she ignored her conscience and answered her sister with as much confidence as she could muster.

"It is merely a note from an acquaintance I happened to make this week." Willa tipped her chin up and swept out of the shop. It would have been a more dramatic exit if she had not been holding half of an iced bun in one hand.

Naturally, Phoebe followed her, pestering Willa with questions about the note. Willa refused to answer any of them, but their noisy conversation aroused Miss Hadfield's suspicions.

"What's this about an acquaintance, Wilhelmina?"

Willa winced at the sound of her full given name, but she pasted a smile on her face when she glanced back over her shoulder. "Oh, only a young lady I met the other day. I am afraid I do not remember her name."

Miss Hadfield raised her eyebrows. "You don't remember her name, but you are exchanging letters with her?" She spoke with the cool suspicion of an experienced governess.

"Not letters," Willa insisted. "Merely a note about looking for each other after church this Sunday."

Then, since both Phoebe and Miss Hadfield were watching her, she cracked open the note and pored over it, doing her best to look nonchalant.

Dear W.S.

I am afraid piety is not one of my virtues. I rarely attend church, but I am happy to do so this week. I will look for you in the churchyard once the service is over, though I may wait until most of the parishioners have departed. I do not like forcing my way through a crowd.

Thank you for telling me how to recognize you! A red cloak, you say? That's an unusual color. I don't own anything quite that distinctive, but I will carry a silver-handled walking stick to help with identification. You might also recognize me by my hair—there are not many people my age who still have blond hair. Usually, it turns to brown by the time one reaches adulthood, or so I have been told. I'm afraid I have not made a study of hair color in humans, though I did once try to develop a system by which to chart the hereditary of coat patterns in barn cats. I gave up that attempt once I realized that female cats in heat will breed with as many toms as they can find, making it quite difficult to ascertain the paternity of their kittens.

You must pardon my digression; sometimes my thoughts move in rather unusual directions. My thinking seems perfectly reasonable to me, but other people have trouble following my line of thought.

Suffice it to say that I will see you on Sunday!

Your friend,
B.R.

The wrinkle in Willa's brow smoothed out when she reached the letter's closing. She had a friend in Dorset! But perhaps not as young a lady as she had hoped, given her rambling about her hair color. She seemed to have a rather eclectic set of interests, too, ranging from horrid novels to heredity.

No matter! Any acquaintance would be a pleasant addition to the family circle. If B.R. were an elderly lady, perhaps she could befriend Mama. And if she were learned in the natural sciences, she might get along quite well with Miss Hadfield, who had always had an interest in botany.

Willa happily folded up the note. She looked up at her sister and her former governess with a bright smile. "All is well! I shall meet my friend after church this Sunday! Only to exchange a quick word, of course. I shan't make you stand around waiting for me."

Once she'd met B.R. face-to-face, they could make arrangements for future meetings. Then, perhaps, Willa would have something more interesting to do than listen to Phoebe recite verses she'd memorized. Phoebe had both a good voice and a good memory, but there were only so many times that one wanted to listen to a recitation of Miss Grammar's latest poem.

Chapter Three

B EN ALMOST DIDN'T make it to church that Sunday. On Friday night, he fell prey to some sort of digestive upset. He stayed up half the night sick to his stomach and loose in his bowels. He worried himself half-sick again trying to figure out how he would let W.S. know why he'd missed their meeting.

But by Saturday afternoon, he felt much better. Aunt Faith insisted on taking his temperature, as if he were a sick child, and he showed no signs of fever.

"Probably just something you ate," she advised him. "You should start off eating bland foods, like beef tea."

Ben stifled a sigh and smiled. "Yes, ma'am. I'll try that." Under other circumstances, he might have argued with her, but he wanted to stay on her good side. She would report back to Grandfather about Ben's recovery, and if she gave a bad report, they might decide Ben needed to stay home on Sunday.

Not that they could have forced him to stay home. Ben was no longer a minor, and even if he had been, Grandfather Marlowe would not have been his legal guardian. But Grandfather had a way of making his "suggestions" seem more like orders. If he ordered his grandson to stay home to convalesce, Ben would be torn about whether to do as his grandfather asked, or what he'd already promised his new friend he would do. He hated decisions like that.

But by Sunday morning, he felt fit as a fiddle, and perfectly capable of walking to St. Clement's parish with his aunt. The church was not far from Marlowe Tower, but Ben rarely bestirred himself to make the walk. He had no particular interest in theology or devotion, and he disliked public events on principle.

The worst of it was that he always had to sit in the best pew, near the front of the church, where the whole congregation could stare at him. And the congregation *did* stare at Ben that Sunday. No doubt they were surprised to see anyone other than Aunt Faith using the Marlowe Tower pew.

Ben had forgotten to bring any lemon drops with him, so he had nothing with which to occupy himself while the clergyman read the lessons for the day in an impressive bass voice. Instead of quietly sucking on a candy, Ben swung his feet back and forth until Aunt Faith silenced him with a stern look, as if he'd been an unruly schoolboy.

After the service ended, he let his aunt leave the pew without him, while he waited for everyone else to exit the church. This was the part of churchgoing he dreaded most. People always wanted to greet their neighbors, stopping to share a word or two with them. Many people stopped Aunt Faith to inquire about Grandfather's health. The parishioners would have been quite willing to chat with Ben, too, if he gave them the chance. But Ben dreaded such idle chit-chat. He had arranged his life to avoid it as much as possible, and he didn't intend to change that now.

Finally, the only person left was the vicar, Mr. Traherne. Ben nodded shyly at him, and when the vicar wished him a good day, he mumbled back an inaudible answer. Then he hurried out of the church before anyone else could catch him and drag him into an unwanted conversation.

His heart pounded as he walked into the churchyard. Goodness, you'd think he was meeting the king! It was only now, though, that Ben realized how very uncomfortable this first meeting might be. He had, rather foolishly, imagined W.S. as a young man of approximately Ben's own age, with similar tastes in books, if not in natural sciences.

But what if W.S. were an old man? Or a boy? Or the sort of wealthy banker or merchant whom his parents would characterize as *nouveau riche*? Ben saw nothing wrong with people who worked for their living, but his father was rather high in the instep. Until this moment, it had never occurred to Ben that he might be about to make what his parents considered an undesirable acquaintance.

He glanced about the churchyard, searching for anyone who could possibly be W.S. In one corner, two women and a child were studying gravestones. One of the women seemed familiar, though he couldn't immediately place her. He felt certain he'd never seen the child before.

Nearer at hand, a young lady in a cloak peered up at the church building, studying the stained glass windows. Ben moved his eyes past her in search of W.S. But there was no one else. He was the only man in the churchyard. Had something delayed W.S.?

As Ben scanned the cemetery again, the bright red of the young lady's cloak caught his eye. *Bright red?* An icy shock washed over him, followed by a flush of embarrassment. It took only a moment for his startling suspicion to become a near-certainty.

Why had he never considered that W.S. might be a woman rather than a man? True, he couldn't think of many women's names that began with W, but there must be some. *Winifred,* he remembered. Maybe her name was "Winifred."

Of course, there was nothing wrong with being a young lady rather than a young man. Winifred S. (or whatever her real name was) might be a perfectly charming, intelligent, well-educated young lady. But she was still a lady. A young lady, so far as he could tell.

Why, he wondered, couldn't she have been an elderly spinster with an interest in literature? In that case, he could have spoken to her as he did his aunts. Or if she had been a child, he could have spoken with her much the same way he would have spoken to one of his younger cousins. Instead, she was a grown woman who looked no older than his own twenty-two years. In other words, far from spinsterhood.

Ben had not always been afraid to talk to women his age. When he'd been a child, conversing with girls had been neither easier nor harder than talking to boys. He'd experienced only his usual difficulties in understanding what other people meant and saying the right thing in response. But as he moved from boyhood into manhood, young women seemed to become both more alluring and more confusing.

A *faux pas* made in interactions with other gentlemen would be bad enough. But somehow, there seemed to be even more potential pitfalls involved when conversing with marriageable young ladies. On top of that, Ben worried that, being marriageable, they might want to marry *him*. His mother had impressed on him the importance of not paying too much attention to a girl if he did not intend to seriously court her. It would not be fair to raise a girl's hopes only to dash them, she said.

Since Ben had no way of telling how much attention might lead a girl to expect a proposal, he preferred to pay as little attention to young ladies as possible. Unfortunately, that wasn't possible today. He'd arranged to meet W.S. and meet her he must. After all, it wasn't her fault that she was a young lady rather than the young man he'd assumed her to be.

He gripped his walking stick more tightly, as if it would somehow protect him from the stranger's feminine charms. He drew a deep breath and took a resolute step towards her.

Hearing his footsteps, she glanced over her shoulder. Some indecipherable emotion flickered across her face, and her mouth fell ajar. She waited for him to approach, her gloved hands clasped at her waist.

When he came to a halt in front of the stranger, he saw that she was biting her lower lip. Oddly, that reassured him. Apparently, he wasn't the only one who felt nervous.

"Are you B.R.?" Her cultured voice hinted at either an expensive education, exposure to good society, or both. Probably not someone his father would stigmatize as a "mushroom," then, Ben concluded.

Up close, he saw she had sky-blue eyes framed by sooty lashes. Strange that she had such eyes when her hair was raven-wing black. In Ben's experience, light-colored eyes most often accompanied light-colored hair.

Deuce take it. W.S. wasn't just a young lady; she was a *pretty* young lady, with delicate eyebrows, a strong chin, and symmetrical features. Her clothing also suggested she came from a wealthy family. That made her precisely the most threatening type of female: one who might view Ben as potential husband material!

Dimly, Ben realized she was still waiting for him to answer. Heat flushed his face. "Yes, I am B.R." He bowed. "W.S., I presume?"

She nodded. "I am Willa Selwyn." Her voice sounded firmer, and she'd lost her initial wide-eyed stare.

"Willow?" Ben wasn't sure he'd heard right. He'd never encountered that name. "As in a willow tree?"

She smiled, showing a glint of pearly teeth. "Not Willow. *Willa.* Short for Wilhelmina."

"Ah, I see." His guess of "William" had not been that far off, then, since Wilhelmina was a feminine form of "Wilhelm," the German version of "William." Somehow, that made him feel a tiny bit less foolish. He hadn't been a hundred percent wrong about every detail.

Just the most important details.

While Ben tried to figure out how to introduce himself, the two women and the child accompanying them turned away from the grave marker they'd been studying and approached Ben and W.S.

The younger of the women wore a slight frown, but the older one's face lit up with pleasure. Now that he was close enough to see the laugh lines around her blue eyes, Ben recognized her as the widow of the previous incumbent of St. Clement's, though it took him a moment to recall her name.

"Mr. Radcliffe!" the gray-haired woman exclaimed. "Good to see you! Why do you make yourself so scarce around here?"

He ignored her rather intrusive question but responded to her greeting. "Good morning, Mrs. Trimmer! I hope you are well?"

"Fine as fivepence, now that my cousin is visiting me. She brought her daughters, as you see." Mrs. Trimmer glanced at the younger woman, who still wore a faint frown. Was that her cousin? They looked nothing alike. Mrs. Trimmer was bony and tall; the younger woman was both shorter and plumper.

"Lady Wilhelmina, Lady Phoebe, Miss Hadfield, may I present Mr. Benjamin Radcliffe? He is Mr. Marlowe's grandson. He moved here a year or two ago to help look after his grandfather."

Ben hastened to make a proper bow.

"Pleased to meet you, Mr. Radcliffe," murmured Miss Hadfield. She wore a prim gray dress, but she had a pleasant face—or rather, one that would have looked pleasant if not for the worry lines. "Have you met Lady Wilhelmina before today?"

Ben's mouth went dry. How could he answer that? Unmarried men and unmarried women were not supposed to correspond. Not unless they were related by blood. He had done wrong in engaging with a correspondence with her. And if she were *Lady* Wilhelmina, she must be the daughter of a nobleman. An earl at the least. *Good Lord!* His stomach sank under the weight of his errors.

Lady Wilhelmina stepped in to answer. "Mr. Radcliffe and I exchanged a word or two in passing, Miss Hadfield, but we were never formally introduced."

The quiet confidence of her voice reassured Ben, making it easier for him to answer. "Yes, that is quite right." He flicked his eyes towards his quondam correspondent and smiled. "It is a pleasure to be properly introduced to you at last, Lady Wilhelmina."

"Oh, I am glad to bring the two of you together!" Mrs. Trimmer gushed. "Back in my husband's time, Ben's mother used to teach in the Sunday school I managed. Of course, in those days she was only Miss Charity Marlowe, not Lady Radcliffe. I've not seen much of dear Miss Charity since she married, since Sir Lewis's estate is in Berkshire. But I'm so glad they could spare Benjamin. It must be difficult to send one's only child off for months at a time—"

Here, Ben interrupted. "You forget, ma'am, that though I did not go to a public school, I did matriculate at Cambridge. That took me well away from home for months at a time, too." He saw no need to mention that he'd left the university without taking a degree.

Mrs. Trimmer, who was every bit as good-natured as he remembered, did not take offense at his correction, saying only, "Oh, yes, I quite forgot that."

Ben glanced at Lady Wilhelmina and smiled wryly. In his reply to her first letter, he had very nearly asked her if she'd gone to university. If he'd done that, he might have learned that W.S. was not the young man he'd been imagining. Not the future friend he'd hoped for. That might have prevented today's disappointment.

Miss Hadfield glanced at the two young ladies. "I am afraid we had best be heading home." She inclined her head at Ben. "I hope to see again, Mr. Radcliffe." Next, she caught Mrs. Trimmer's eye and raised her eyebrows, though Ben had no idea what message she meant to convey.

Fortunately, Mrs. Trimmer seemed to know what was expected of her. "Thursday afternoon is my usual day for calling, but Benjamin knows he is welcome to drop in any day of the week. And bring your aunt if you can, Mr. Radcliffe." Mrs. Trimmer patted his arm.

Ben, who hated being touched by strangers, could not prevent the flinch that followed. He hoped she did not notice.

Though it went against the grain, Ben said, "I shall have to call one of these days, then."

What a ridiculous idea! Morning calls were for women. He could imagine few things worse than sipping tea and swapping gossip with locals in Mrs. Trimmer's parlor. He'd better find a way to avoid such a visit.

Chapter Four

M ISS HADFIELD WAITED until Phoebe was happily playing in the back garden and Cousin Sarah was in her room napping before she spoke to Willa about the meeting in the churchyard.

"Willa, please help me with this mending."

The polite request did not fool Willa for even a second. The mending was only a pretext for the scolding she was about to receive. Still, Phoebe's clothes did need to be mended. Neither Willa nor Mama had brought a lady's maid with them to handle such chores, and it was not fair to leave all the work to Miss Hadfield.

Willa picked up one of Phoebe's pinafores and threaded her needle. She had some idea of what her former governess meant to say, but she preferred to wait for her to speak rather than rushing in with excuses.

"I would like to know what you meant when you said that you had exchanged a few words with Mr. Radcliffe." Miss Hadfield spoke placidly, and her eyes kept following the movement of her needle.

But Willa heard the keen steel edge behind Miss Hadfield's question. She bit her lip, struggling to contain all the excuses and objections she wanted to make. The warmth of Cousin Sarah's welcome and her invitation to call showed that there could be no harm in Mr. Radcliffe. Even so, Willa swallowed uneasily.

"I am waiting for your answer, my dear." Miss Hadfield's voice remained as gentle as ever. She rarely needed to raise her voice to hold her pupils' attention.

Willa put down her mending with a sigh. "Since coming to Newell, I've been so very bored. One day, I wrote a letter, put it in a bottle, and tossed it off Castle Rock Point. Mr. Radcliffe found it and answered my letter. That is all."

"And you encountered him after church entirely by chance?" Miss Hadfield caught Willa's gaze and raised her eyebrows.

A flush heated Willa's face. "We made an arrangement to meet," she mumbled. "But—"

Miss Hadfield cut her off before she could say another word in explanation. "Wilhelmina Selwyn, do you mean to say that you arranged a clandestine meeting with a *young man?*" She invested the words "young man" with as much contempt as if she had said "criminal" or "highwayman."

Willa's face burned with shame, but she did not look away. "I thought he was a girl." Her blush would have deepened, if that were possible. "What I mean is, we did not sign our full names in the notes. Just initials." She twisted her fingers together anxiously, knowing how ridiculous it sounded. "I only knew that I was corresponding with someone called B.R. I didn't think to ask how old or young B.R. was, or whether they were a man or woman. I assumed I was writing to a lady, though I don't know why."

She did know why, though. She had been hoping for a friend, someone who could enter into her interests and keep her company. Mr. Radcliffe might be a fine, upstanding gentleman, but she could not gossip and giggle with him as she'd imagined.

Miss Hadfield set aside her own mending. She rested her chin on one hand for a long, thoughtful moment. "I see that you have already realized how foolish your assumptions were," she said gently. "But do you understand how close you came to scandal? You maintained a clandestine correspondence with a young gentleman, then snuck around behind our backs to meet him in secret!"

"I did not!" The heat in Willa's face now came from anger. "I deliberately chose a public place to meet. Just in case. . . in case something went wrong." Cousin Sarah and Miss Hadfield had been only yards away the whole time.

"So you *did* know you were doing something dangerous." Miss Hadfield did not wait for an answer. "It was well for you that you chose to meet in the churchyard. If you had met him in some lonely, isolated spot, he could have done anything to you. You could have been hurt. Or ruined."

Willa gulped. "I don't think he is the sort of person who would do something so wicked," she whispered. "He only wanted someone to ride with him in the park. His grandfather's park, I mean. And he was going to share his books with me." A murderer would not offer to loan her *Frankenstein*, would he?

"No, I imagine he's no murderer. Mrs. Trimmer has only good things to say about him," Miss Hadfield grudgingly admitted. "He seems to come from a very respectable family. Heir to a baronetcy, to boot." She darted an odd, sideways look at Willa.

"What does being heir to a baronetcy have to do with anything?" Willa protested. She blushed again when she finally realized what Miss Hadfield meant. "He wasn't there to *court* me, Haddy! He didn't even know I was a young lady."

"You *think* he didn't know," Miss Hadfield retorted. "He might have figured it out somehow. Though he looks a little young to be on the hunt for a wife. I ought to ask your cousin if she knows how old he is."

"Oh, no!" In her mortification, Willa could only stare at the floor. "I am sure he did not think of me in the light of. . . of a potential bride. We were only going to ride and talk about books together."

"And he might not be objectionable as a companion, Willa. But if you ride with him, you must take a groom with you as a chaperone. And you are not to exchange further letters with him, whether by bottle or by post. At least not until you are betrothed." She fixed a stern look on Willa.

Willa buried her face in her hands, not sure whether to laugh or cry. Miss Hadfield stubbornly persisted in discussing B.R. as a potential suitor, but that wasn't what Willa wanted at all! She had only wanted a friend.

"I wish I'd never heard of Benjamin Radcliffe," she grumbled.

"Now that is nonsense." The governess spoke briskly as she picked up her mending, suggesting she had finished her lecture. "You knew perfectly well when you came to Newell that there was no guarantee you would meet any eligible young men here, let alone a handsome man who shares your interests. You ought to consider yourself fortunate."

Willa laughed bitterly. "Haddy, you can't have it both ways! You can't claim that it was terribly improper for me to meet Mr. Radcliffe, then turn around and congratulate me on the new acquaintance."

The governess smiled. "On the contrary, both things can be true at the same time. Even an improper action may have beneficial results. But mind, you are not to go running after Mr. Radcliffe. If he wishes to encounter you again, he will make it happen."

"Yes, Miss Hadfield." Willa picked up her needle again and resumed mending. She felt certain Miss Hadfield misunderstood the situation, but she had no idea how to convince Haddy that Mr. Radcliffe had no intention of courting Willa. For all she knew, he might not plan on seeing her again at all.

BUT WILLA WAS proven wrong on Thursday afternoon. That day, Mama felt well enough to leave her room again. She lounged on the sofa, a fashion journal in hand. Willa sat at the writing table in the corner of the parlor, writing a letter to one of her uncles. She had so little news to share that it was hard to fill a page.

Uncle Rowland's news from London was always more interesting than anything Willa could write, anyway. As secretary to the Marquis of Reading, he heard both the latest political developments and the spiciest *on-dits*. He had a gift for retelling an anecdote, too, which he put to good use in the newspaper column he wrote under a pseudonym.

Meanwhile, Willa could think of nothing better to write than that the sky was grayer today than yesterday.

Phoebe stood before the window, peering out in the hopes of spotting a passing dog, so she was the one who first noticed the visitors. "There's a carriage here!" she squealed. "A carriage with a coat of arms!"

"It is hardly surprising for a carriage to bear a coat of arms," Miss Hadfield observed. But she rose to her feet and peered around the curtain. "Ah," she said in a tone of deep satisfaction, "it is young Mr. Radcliffe, and I suspect that lady accompanying him is his aunt." She rested a hand on Phoebe's shoulder. "Phoebe, I believe you and I ought to go practice penmanship in the dining room and leave this room to the grown-ups."

"Why don't I ever get to talk to the interesting guests?" Phoebe whined.

Miss Hadfield gentled her voice. "Because you are still a schoolgirl. But you have only a few years left before you come out."

Willa smiled at her sister. "Enjoy childhood while you can," she advised. "There are even more rules you have to follow once you grow up."

Rules about who you could spend time with, and for how long, and in what settings, for example. Rules about what to wear for every occasion, with the risk of being labelled a "quiz" if one chose poorly. Rules—her disgruntled thoughts came to a halt when the housemaid opened the parlor door.

"Miss Marlowe and Mr. Radcliffe," she announced.

The guests stepped into the room, and everyone turned to greet them. Miss Marlowe, a tall woman whose hair had begun to gray, walked with a sturdy wooden cane. She gently elbowed her nephew, prompting him to bow.

"It is good to see you out and about, Miss Marlowe. Won't you take a seat?" Cousin Sarah glanced at Mama, who responded with a subtle nod. "Lady Inglewhite, may I present Miss Marlowe, of Marlowe Tower, and her nephew, Benjamin? Mr. Radcliffe, I should say."

"It is a pleasure to meet you." Mama might have said more had not a fit of coughing overtaken her. "I beg you will forgive my cough. We were all of us quite ill some weeks ago, and I have yet to make a full recovery."

"I know well how that goes." Miss Marlowe grimaced in sympathy. "My own health is rather uncertain, at best."

"Won't you please take a seat?" Cousin Sarah gestured to the few remaining armchairs. The sitting room, like most of the house, was on the smaller side, but it had been elegantly furnished with modern rosewood furnishings.

Willa expected Mr. Radcliffe to sit next to her, so they could easily talk to each other. Instead, he sat in the chair nearest the door, as if he wanted to be able to escape in a hurry if the conversation went south. He sat stiffly, looking as uncomfortable as a child forced into paying a call with his elders.

How odd! Could he be younger than he looked? Willa had guessed he was about her age, if not a little older. She studied him surreptitiously and came to the same conclusion. Tall and well-muscled from his riding and walking, "B.R." certainly looked like a grown man rather than a youth.

And, she admitted to herself, Miss Hadfield was right about him being handsome. Threads of gold glinted in his dark-blond hair, and though she sat too far to see his eyes well, she clearly remembered their vivid-green color. If Mr. Radcliffe were dressed in evening clothes and dropped into a London ballroom, debutantes would swoon!

"I will not take up too much of your time, Mrs. Trimmer," Miss Marlowe said. "I am sure having houseguests keeps you busy. But I wanted to extend an invitation to dine with us this Saturday. Of course, your guests are most welcome to join us!" She nodded politely in the direction of Lady Inglewhite, then turned her head to include Willa in the gesture.

Willa darted a glance at Mr. Radcliffe, but he was still staring down at his feet. She felt increasingly confused. She had initially assumed that he'd called to see her again, but he hadn't spoken a word. She wasn't sure he'd even so much as looked her in the face. He couldn't really be *that* shy, could he?

Cousin Sarah glanced at Mama, asking a silent question with a lift of her brows. Mama nodded in response.

"I am afraid my health does not permit me to dine out yet," Mama said graciously. "But I am certain my daughter would love to accompany Mrs. Trimmer." A pointed look at Willa made it clear which response Mama expected.

"Indeed, I would be delighted to accept your invitation, Miss Marlowe." Willa hesitated, not certain whether she should admit that she already had some acquaintance with Mr. Radcliffe. Did his aunt know about the letters they'd exchanged?

Mr. Radcliffe cleared his throat. "You might enjoy looking at my collection of artifacts from the beach, Miss—Lady Wilhelmina, I mean. I would be happy to show them to you. And to Mrs. Trimmer, of course."

He finally looked Willa in the eye. But he looked pained, as if he didn't really want to see her at Marlowe Tower. Willa's heart sank, and her smile faltered, though she promptly forced it back into place.

"Splendid!" Her feigned enthusiasm didn't sound convincing even to herself.

Chapter Five

AUNT FAITH SANK down on the worn cushioning of the old carriage and sighed with relief. Ben could only suppose that her arthritis was acting up.

"Benjamin Radcliffe, one would think you had never paid a call on a neighbor," she scolded. "Where are your manners, young man?"

Ben hung his head. "It was an awkward situation."

Speaking to Lady Wilhemina by herself would have been bad enough. She was a young lady, yes, but she was also W.S. Their brief exchange of letters might have paved the way for a conversation. But he couldn't discuss their clandestine correspondence in front of Lady Inglewhite, who might or might not know that her daughter had been corresponding with a young bachelor.

Conversing with the countess posed its own challenges, since he knew nothing about her other than that she was currently recovering from influenza. Probably he should have uttered some trite comments about the weather, the healthfulness of sea bathing, or the most recent discovery of a fossil. Or were fossils considered unladylike? Surely not, given Miss Anning's success finding and selling them! Many holiday trippers bought fossils as souvenirs of their visit to the Dorset coast.

"I hope you will be more sociable when the ladies dine with

us," Ben's aunt continued. "I only asked them on your account, you know. Neither your grandfather nor I particularly care for entertaining strangers."

Ben stared blankly at Aunt Faith. "When did I ever ask you to host a dinner party?" He liked dinner parties even less than his grandfather did!

"You said you wanted to get to know this Lady What's-her-name." Her gentle voice carried a faint hint of rebuke.

"Oh." Had he said that? He had wanted to befriend W.S. when he thought W.S. was a man, but given the reality—well, circumstances made such a friendship impractical.

"Thank you for thinking of me," Ben concluded, though he was certain that dining with Mrs. Trimmer and her cousin would be a disaster.

ON FRIDAY NIGHT, Ben went to bed silently hoping for a rainstorm that would force his aunt to cancel tomorrow's dinner party. He would even be willing to undergo a second round of dyspepsia if that meant being left in peace! But he had no such luck. Though clouds hovered over the coast all day, no rain fell to alter anyone's plans.

In fact, Lady Wilhelmina and her cousin arrived early. Aunt Faith, dressed in her customary black silk, rose to greet them. "How lovely you both look! Lady Wilhelmina, that is such a charming confection of a gown! I only wish our simple entertainments were more worthy of your finery."

While Ben bowed, he doubtfully examined the guests' attire. Mrs. Trimmer wore a simply cut gown, in a practical dove gray. But "confection" was a good word for Lady Wilhelmina's dress, which had two layers: an opaque layer of some shiny fabric, topped by a layer of embroidered see-through fabric.

Aunt Faith glanced at Ben and raised a single eyebrow.

Though he sometimes missed social signals, he knew perfectly well what *that* meant. He was supposed to say something complimentary, too.

"Yes, you do both look very well this evening." Then, feeling that something more ought to be said, he asked, "Is that muslin?"

A smile flashed across Lady Wilhemina's face, but she repressed it as she shook her head. "It is silk net, Mr. Radcliffe. Silk is all the rage for evening gowns these days."

"Whatever it is, it looks lovely." He wished he'd kept his mouth shut rather than exposing his ignorance. But how was he supposed to know what fabrics were in style?

Especially since what he really thought about the dress was that it would not be practical for walking down to the carriage house. He'd hoped to show W.S. his collection of treasures from the beach, but she probably wouldn't want to venture into the stable yard while wearing a delicate white silk dress.

But Lady Wilhelmina unexpectedly brought the subject up herself. "What is that rock you have on the mantel?" She squinted at it from across the room. "Is it a souvenir from a holiday trip?"

"That's one of your fossils, isn't it, Ben?" Aunt Faith looked pointedly at him, as if he were a child who needed to be prompted to talk about his latest toy.

Ben lifted his chin. He was a grown man, and he was perfectly capable of discussing his interests. Talking about *other people's* interests was the real challenge.

"Yes, it's a fossil. An ammonite. I found it when I visited Lyme Regis a few years ago. There aren't as many fossils here at Castle Rock Cove, but you find a few every now and again." He carefully lifted the specimen and brought it to Lady Wilhelmina. "You can see it much better from up close."

She held the fossil carefully as she turned it around, studying it from different angles. "Oh, how fascinating! I thought it would look like a snail shell, but it's quite different, isn't it?"

"People used to call them snakestones," Ben explained, "because they thought ammonites were coiled-up snakes that had turned into stone. In the north of England, there were legends of a saint turning all the snakes into stone."

Her eyes lit up. "Oh yes! St. Hilda! I remember reading about that in *Marmion*. Just as well that it's only a legend. It would be rather sad for the poor snakes, if it were true!" She wrinkled her nose, then looked up at Ben. "Do you think it hurt the ammonites to be turned into fossils?"

Ben had never thought about that. "Surely they must have been dead before they were fossilized?" he suggested. "That's what I've always assumed."

"How do you know they were ever alive?" Mrs. Trimmer wanted to know. "Couldn't that simply be a pretty pattern on the rocks?"

"A good question," Ben admitted. "The resemblance between the spiral pattern in the stone and the shells of certain living invertebrates, such as the nautilus, suggests that ammonites were once alive, for one, and—"

At that fortuitous moment, Graves opened the drawing room door and announced, "Dinner is served."

Ben silently escorted Lady Wilhelmina to the table, relieved that he'd been cut off before he had a chance to bore her with an unwanted geology lecture.

Only after he sat down did it occur to him that etiquette might have required him to escort Mrs. Trimmer, who was so much Lady Wilhelmina's senior. He tensed up for a panicked moment until he remembered that Lady Wilhelmina outranked a clergyman's widow. He had done right.

"The spiral pattern on the ammonite really is quite pretty," Lady Wilhelmina said. "Did people incorporate ammonites into rococo furniture design, do you think?"

Though Ben knew next to nothing about rococo design, Aunt Faith knew a bit, and Grandfather Marlowe knew even more, so that supplied a topic of conversation for the first half of dinner.

After that, Mrs. Trimmer asked Grandfather a question about the dairy on the home farm. Ben blithely ignored the conversation, returning his attention to the dinner itself. He hated trying to eat and talk at the same time, so it was a relief to be able to focus on his food and drink.

He did not get a chance to speak to Lady Wilhelmina alone until after dinner, when Graves brought tea and coffee to the drawing room.

"Do you have many fossils?" she asked brightly.

"Only a few. I am actually more interested in the man-made objects one finds on the beach. Things like old coins, odds and ends from shipwrecks, and of course sea glass."

"And letters in a bottle?" Her mouth remained set in a serious line, but the hint of a smile twinkled in her eyes as she leaned forward.

Though Lady Wilhelmina moved only a fraction of an inch closer, Ben's heart beat faster. He fumbled with his cup, splashing coffee onto his trousers. He had no idea whether the blush burning along his cheekbones was due to his unexpected clumsiness, or if it was a reaction to Lady Wilhelmina's physical proximity. He felt entirely too aware of how attractive she was.

"Oh no! Here, let me help!" Lady Wilhelmina attempted to help by dabbing at the stain, but since that meant dabbing at his pants, this escalated the awkwardness by the power of ten.

Ben yanked the napkin away from her before she could accidentally touch something infinitely more embarrassing than his leg.

Her eyes widened as she drew back from him. "I'm sorry. I was only trying to help."

"Oh, it's quite all right. I mean, I can take care of it. I never liked these trousers, anyway." He cleared his throat and forced himself to look her in the eyes. "You were saying?"

"I'm afraid I've forgotten. I'm sure it was nothing of any importance." She stared down at her own neatly folded hands, looking embarrassed.

Perfect! They were both absolutely mortified. To make matters worse, Ben kept imaging what it would have felt like if she *had* touched his groin while trying to clean up the spill. Such contact would undoubtedly be stimulating, even with two layers of clothing separating them.

Desperate to turn his mind to a safer subject, Ben blurted out, "If it weren't so late, I would show you some of the objects I've collected on the beach. But I don't suppose we can go out to the stable at this hour."

They both glanced towards the night-darkened windows. "It is a pity," Lady Wilhelmina said, but he could not tell if she meant it, or if it was merely a social fiction.

"You would be welcome to call on us some afternoon," Aunt Faith suggested. "We do not keep regular hours for callers, but we would always welcome a visit from such an old friend as Mrs. Trimmer, wouldn't we, Papa?" She looked towards Ben's grandfather, giving a jerk of her chin to indicate that he should back her up.

Grandfather Marlowe must have been half-asleep in his chair. Hearing himself addressed, he startled, then blinked owlishly at Aunt Faith. "Oh, of course. You are welcome to have all the callers you want, Faith. But I thought you preferred writing letters to entertaining visitors—"

Aunt Faith loudly interrupted her brother. "Even a hermit needs to see a friendly face now and again! We would love to have you here, Mrs. Trimmer. You too, Lady Wilhelmina. Wouldn't you agree, Benjamin?"

"Er, yes?" He relaxed a trifle when his aunt's pleased expression showed this must have been the right answer. He shifted his eyes towards Lady Wilhelmina and forced a smile. "If you call during the day, I can show you my collection."

The smile fell away from his aunt's face, and she subtly shook her head at him. He recognized that look, though he didn't know what he'd done wrong this time.

"That is, if you want to," he amended. "The sea glass and some of the shells are rather pretty." Girls liked pretty things, didn't they?

"That would be charming," Lady Wilhelmina replied.

Ben suspected she was merely being polite. Very likely, some excuse would prevent her from calling with her cousin. And that was just as well, wasn't it? She and Ben could have nothing to say to each other.

Chapter Six

"Mama," Willa asked, "do you think a friendship can exist between a gentleman and a lady?"

"Of course." Mama once again reclined on the sofa, this time with a popular scandal-rag for entertainment. "I am friends with both your uncles, aren't I?"

Willa made a face. That didn't count! Uncle Rowland and Uncle Richard were family, not friends. "But have you ever been friends with a gentleman who wasn't part of your family?"

"Hmm." Mama turned the pages of her newspaper. "Yes, I have had gentlemen friends. When I was much younger, I was quite good friends with a fellow named Sir Horatio Bradford. He had no interest in marriage, but he had many friends who were women." She sighed. "He always knew the juiciest *on-dits* before anyone else did."

"Like Uncle Rowland?" Willa suggested.

Her mother chuckled. "Apart from both having a good ear for gossip, their personalities and interests were quite different." She hesitated, a thoughtful look on her face. "I suppose they were also similar in that that they both had a very close particular friend. But what makes you ask about friendship?"

Willa looked down at her embroidery, pretending to be concerned about the evenness of her stitches. "No reason."

"Is this about the young man up at Marlowe Tower?" Mama

asked.

"Of course not. It was merely an idle question." But Willa's blush gave the lie to her words. She most certainly *was* thinking about Mr. Radcliffe. Ever since the dinner party, she'd wondered if the two of them might have a friendship after all, even though he wasn't the young lady she had imagined.

"I see." Mama smiled in that knowing, parental way that always annoyed Willa. "There is no harm in forming some new acquaintances while we are here. One never knows when one may need a friend."

"Quite right," Willa agreed, though she didn't think her mother had given a very satisfactory answer to her question.

At least Mama didn't seem opposed to her pursuing an acquaintanceship with Mr. Radcliffe. Maybe Willa would find out for herself whether a gentleman and a lady could be friends.

ON THE LAST day of April, Willa and Cousin Sarah paid their promised call at Marlowe Tower. Willa assumed she would find Mr. Radcliffe there, but when the butler ushered them into the drawing room, they found only his aunt.

"Benjamin is out in his workroom," Miss Marlowe explained. "It's in the loft above the carriage house. If you like, Rosie can take you there. I know Benjamin was hoping to show you his collection."

Willa blinked. Was Miss Marlowe suggesting that Willa tour Mr. Radcliffe's collection without a chaperone? How very improper! But when she glanced uncertainly at Cousin Sarah, the older woman nodded her encouragement.

"Go on, dear," Cousin Sarah urged. "That way, Miss Marlowe and I can have a comfortable coze without boring you with our gossip."

"I'm sure I wouldn't be bored." Willa, who was not the least bit interested in Newell gossip, spoke purely for politeness' sake. She was quite happy to follow the housemaid out to the stables.

A tall row of holly trees hid the stable block, which was larger than she expected. It was just as well that she had a guide. Rosie politely showed Willa to the staircase leading to the loft above the carriage house, then stepped back. "It's the only room up there, so you can't miss it," she explained.

"Thank you." Willa tried to hide her surprise when the maid turned and walked away. She had assumed that Rosie would keep her company, for the sake of propriety.

As she climbed the stairs, Willa's mouth felt dry. This visit, which had seemed so promising, now felt like a very bad idea. What was she doing here? It wasn't as if she were really interested in fossils or seashells. Maybe it wasn't too late to turn around and go back. But how would she explain that to Miss Marlowe?

"Arf! Arf!" A sharp bark took the decision out of her hands.

"What is it, Cato?" The door swung open, revealing Mr. Radcliffe and a curly coated dog of unidentifiable breed. "Oh! Lady Wilhelmina!"

Well might he sound surprised, Willa thought sourly. Mr. Radcliffe clearly wasn't prepared to receive guests. He had taken off his morning coat, revealing a green-striped waistcoat over a linen shirt.

More shocking yet, he had rolled his shirtsleeves nearly up to his elbows. Willa's eyes were drawn to his forearms. She could not remember the last time she'd seen a gentleman without a coat on.

Mr. Radcliffe broke the silence. "Er, I suppose you are here to see my collection?" He stepped aside and gestured for her to enter the room.

Willa stepped in, doing her best to shape her expression into a look of scholarly interest. In truth, fossils and seashells did not interest her nearly as much as Mr. Radcliffe's state of undress. While he talked about geodes and sea glass, she kept taking surreptitious glances at his bare arms. When he came to a halt in front of the window, the afternoon light gilded the tiny hairs on his arms. Or were they already golden, like the hair on his head?

Unfortunately, Willa's glances must not have been surreptitious enough. Mr. Radcliffe caught her looking at him.

"Is there something wrong with—oh! I forgot to put my coat back on. One moment, please!"

Rosy color rushed to his face, highlighting his prominent cheekbones. He turned away and grabbed the dark-blue coat draped over the back of a chair. He kept his back to her as he shrugged it on, giving her the distinct impression that he was avoiding her gaze.

While he repaired his dress, Willa glanced around the room. She had expected it to be full of glass curiosity shelves, but there were only a couple of those. Instead, the room was dominated by walls of shelves and a large apothecary cabinet.

When Mr. Radcliffe turned back around, he looked disappointingly respectable again. Only a flush along his cheekbones hinted at his discomposure.

"My apologies, Lady Wilhemina," he said. "As I was saying, I am more interested in man-made objects that wash up on the beach, but sometimes natural artifacts catch my eye. Like this did, today." He gestured towards the table in the center of the room.

Willa peered down at the black cloth square in the center of the table. She expected to see a pretty seashell. What she found instead made her cover her mouth with surprise.

"A seahorse! So tiny!" And, sadly, very dead. Poor thing!

"I found it washed up on the beach this morning," Mr. Radcliffe explained. "I've seen them before, but not in such good condition."

Willa wrinkled her brow. "What will you do with it? Bury it?"

"Bury it? Oh, no. They dry very well. After it dries out entirely, I shall add it to my specimen case. See, I already have a few sea stars." He gestured to the display case set up along the wall.

Willa pretended to admire the bits of coral and dried starfish. What really caught her attention, though, was a jar full of sweets on a shelf near the table.

"You must like peppermint," she suggested.

"Hmm?" He looked in the direction she pointed and shrugged. "Oh, my Aunt Patience sent us those. I do like boiled sweets, but I prefer lemon drops or barley sugar. My grandfather is the one who loved peppermints, but his dentist told him they were damaging his teeth. He gives them to me instead."

He lifted the stopper and took one out. "Would you care for one?"

"Oh, yes, thank you." She popped it into her mouth. As the cool flavor flooded across her tongue, she looked about the room. A glint of green in one of the glass cases caught her attention.

"Oh, that must be the sea glass!" She hurried across the room to take a look, and Mr. Radcliffe followed her.

The whole case was full of sea glass: mostly green, blue, and white, with a few bits of black and amber glass mixed in.

"Yes, these are all pieces I found either down at the cove or on Newell Beach." He lifted the glass lid and took out a lovely bit of cobalt blue. "This is the most perfectly shaped teardrop I've ever found. Usually, sea glass is more irregular in form."

He handed the teardrop to Willa so she could examine it more closely. She held it up to the light of the window. As sunlight streamed through the little jewel, her mouth fell open in awe.

"How pretty!" To Willa, this was far more interesting than dead seahorses or starfish.

Mr. Radcliffe's eyes widened, too. "Look—no, I suppose you can't see. I haven't any looking glasses in here. But the color of that sea glass matches your eyes almost exactly. Quite the coincidence."

Willa blinked, not at all certain how to respond. Was that a compliment? Or merely an observation? She decided to treat it as the latter. Mr. Radcliffe had spoken matter-of-factly. He did not sound as if he were trying to flatter her.

"You could make a charming piece of jewelry with this," she

suggested. "A pendant, for example. I imagine it would be easy to do." It might be as simple as wrapping the glass drop with wire and attaching it to a chain.

He shrugged. "I suppose so. I know nothing about jewelry, my lady. I shall leave the jewelry making to you."

She handed the pretty bauble back and watched somewhat wistfully as he carefully returned it to the case.

"I am sure I could make something interesting with glass like that," she agreed. "It's a pity I can't collect sea glass for myself."

"Oh, but you can," he assured her. "It's easy. All you need do is wait for the tide to go out, then walk along the beach. You should stay away from the cliffs to avoid rock falls, though."

Willa shook her head. Rock falls were the least of her problem. "I do not care for walking along the beach. I hate the ocean." She wrinkled her nose and confessed, "That's part of why this long visit to the seaside is so dreadful for me."

"You *hate* the ocean?" A puzzled line formed on his forehead. "Why?"

She drew a deep breath, knowing from experience that he wouldn't understand, no matter what she said. No one ever did. But fortune intervened in the form of a scratch at the door. Mr. Radcliffe hurried over to open it.

It was the same maidservant who'd shown Willa the way to the carriage house. "Lady Wilhelmina? Your cousin is wishful to go back into town now."

"Oh, yes, I will be there in a trice," Willa promised. She turned to take leave of her host. "Thank you very much for showing me your collection, Mr. Radcliffe. It was most interesting." At least, some of it was.

Mr. Radcliffe looked surprised. "Oh, must you go so soon? I didn't even get to show you the sea pottery I've found."

Sea pottery? She'd never even heard of that. Willa bit her lip and thought quickly. "I mustn't keep my cousin waiting. Perhaps I can return another day?" She was always looking for ways to occupy her time, since she wasn't interested in sea bathing.

"Yes, you'll have to come back some time," he agreed. "Maybe next week?"

"Oh, yes, maybe." Willa waited for a moment, expecting that he would escort her back to the house, but instead he sat down at the table and reached for a notebook.

She took that as her dismissal and hurried back to the house. Despite what she'd said, she doubted she'd get to return to the room above the carriage house. Cousin Sarah might have been willing to let her explore it without a chaperone today, but Willa knew better than to expect that to happen again. Even if it were possible for a lady to develop a friendship with a gentleman, propriety would always impose a barrier between them.

Chapter Seven

B EN GOT QUITE a bit of work done that afternoon, despite the interruption of a guest. He cataloged today's finding, doing his best to sketch the seahorse in his notebook. He had never had proper drawing lessons—a lack he sorely regretted. A natural historian who could not accurately sketch specimens would have difficulty sharing his findings with others.

Still, he thought his ability with a pencil had improved a good deal. His first attempt to sketch a seashell looked like the work of a nursery child, but his current attempts might pass for the work of a schoolgirl.

Did Lady Wilhelmina know how to draw? Ben laid down his pencil and stared unseeingly out the window as he wondered. He ought to have asked her whether she had any artistic abilities. Many ladies did study drawing and painting.

His friend Mr. Sanders had been fortunate enough to marry a woman who passed her artistic ability on to her daughters. The eldest Miss Sanders had grown up helping her father record the seashells he found. The father-daughter collaboration ultimately resulted in a pretty book about the beaches of Devon. Sanders had published it as a labor of love, but it sold surprisingly well.

For a moment, Ben imagined what it would be like to have an artist on hand with whom he could collaborate. There must be a book's worth of discoveries to be made right here at Castle

Rock Cove.

"Pfft!" He dismissed that pleasant fantasy and forced himself to look at the reality, which was a seahorse sketch that only a child would be proud of. Still, it was better than what he could have drawn a year ago. By this time next year, he might do better yet.

He set aside his notebook and pencil, reaching instead for the writing desk he used for his correspondence. Thinking of Sanders had reminded Ben that he owed his friend a letter.

Halfway through the letter, some whim made him add, "Do you happen to know anything about making jewelry out of sea glass? I found a particularly lovely bit of blue glass that I thought might do well as a pendant."

A whine at the door reminded Ben that it was past time for Cato's afternoon walk. He set the letter aside to be finished later and thought no more about either sketching or jewelry.

THE EVENING AFTER Lady Wilhelmina and her cousin called at Marlowe Tower, Ben's pleasant day took a turn for the worse when his stomach started cramping. Again? Hadn't he dealt with dyspepsia just a couple of weeks ago? He did not understand how he could have gotten sick so soon after the last incident.

Ben drank a cup of peppermint tea, at his aunt's suggestion, and went to bed early. But he woke up less than hour later, when his nausea turned into vomiting.

The rest of the night was a horrible fog of nausea, cramping, and vomiting, followed by diarrhea. The latter symptom sent him downstairs to the water closet. After what seemed like an eternity of painful intestinal purging, he collapsed outside the water closet.

The cool wooden floor of the corridor soothed Ben's body, exhausted from having so violently emptied itself. He closed his eyes, intending to rest for a moment or two to gain the strength needed to haul himself upstairs.

Instead, he fell asleep. Hours later, the shriek of a startled housemaid jolted him awake.

"Wha??" The foul taste in Ben's mouth turned his stomach, his neck hurt from the angle at which he'd slept, and his night-shirt stank. The only good thing that could be said about his condition was that he was no longer violently emptying his digestive tract.

He stood up on legs so shaky, he had to lean against the wall for support. His hands and feet must have fallen asleep, too, because he felt the familiar pins-and-needles sensation of a limb that has lain in one position too long.

"Master Benjamin, should I wake your aunt up?" Rosie asked. "You look terrible."

"I smell terrible, too," Ben muttered. "You had better fetch Miss Marlowe."

Naturally, his aunt fussed over him. She forced more of her home remedies on him when all he wanted was a cup of tea. The medicine she gave him this morning tasted far nastier than last night's pleasantly flavored peppermint tea.

"I do hope you aren't going to inherit your grandfather's dyspepsia. It can make life miserable." Aunt Faith dabbed at Ben's face with a wet cloth, as if he were incapable of cleaning himself up.

"Auntie, it is merely an upset stomach. Probably something I ate. And I am still capable of washing myself." He took the cloth out of her hand.

"But your grandfather and I ate everything you did yester-day," she argued, "and neither of us are unwell. Why, just yesterday, Papa told me he thought Dr. Milner's new treatment was successful, for he hadn't had dyspepsia in days."

"I'm happy to hear it," Ben muttered.

Problem was, he'd heard it before. Every time Grandfather Marlowe went more than a few days without discomfort, he announced that his dyspepsia had been cured. Every time, he was proven wrong when his symptoms eventually returned.

"I had better send for the doctor," Aunt Faith decided.

This time, Ben did not argue. He doubted Dr. Milner could do more than ease his symptoms, but sending for him would hurt nothing but Grandfather's pocket. Easing Aunt Faith's mind would be worth the cost.

Sure enough, when Dr. Milner arrived, he diagnosed Ben with something he called "gastritis." He prescribed a colic treatment, the primary ingredient of which was laudanum.

Ben made a face when he heard Dr. Milner's prescription. Perhaps some people enjoyed taking laudanum, but he hated the way the drug made him feel.

Unfortunately, Aunt Faith did not care about his preferences. After a servant returned from the apothecary with a bottle of the prescribed medicine, Ben's aunt showed up in his doorway armed with a measuring spoon and a determined expression.

"You heard the doctor," she said firmly. "You had better have a dose of this colic medicine. It will calm your stomach."

Ben took it, if only because he felt too weak to argue. If he hadn't been so sick, he would have pointed out that he was capable of deciding for himself which medicines to take. But then, if he had been well, his aunt wouldn't have tried to make him take the nostrum in the first place, would she?

He fell asleep still trying to figure out whether there was a golden mean between being too sick to argue and too healthy to need medication. Unfortunately for his side of the debate, the laudanum proved helpful. He slept very well indeed.

THE NEXT DAY, Ben felt a good deal better. His digestive organs had ceased rebelling, so he refused to take another dose of the colic treatment. This time, his aunt respected his wishes. But she insisted that he needed time to recover from his sickness, and she refused to let Ben eat anything more demanding than beef tea and dry toast.

The next day, Aunt Faith entered his room, wearing a broad smile. "I have a surprise for you, Ben," she announced.

"Is that it that new book about shipwrecks off the coast of Cornwall?" he asked hopefully. He had ordered the book directly from the publisher, but it seemed to be delayed.

Aunt Faith's smile faltered. "Well, no. It's not a book. Not exactly."

Ben stared at her, waiting for her to elaborate. Instead, she merely shrugged. Then she studied Ben intently. "Maybe you should comb your hair first."

Definitely not a book, then. Aunt Faith would only worry about Ben's appearance if someone were going to see him, which meant that the surprise was. . . a better physician? An unexpected visit from King George?

Not quite. It was only Mrs. Trimmer and her cousin, Lady Wilhelmina.

"I thought Willa might like to read to you," Mrs. Trimmer suggested. "She is very good at reading aloud."

"I can read for myself," Ben explained. "There is nothing wrong with my eyesight."

His aunt glared at him, as if he'd said something horrifically rude. Had he said something wrong? But what he'd said was perfectly true! He'd had an upset stomach, which seemed to have passed already, and it hadn't affected his ability to read at all.

"We don't have to read. That was only a suggestion, you know."

Lady Wilhelmina's apologetic tone finally clued Ben in. She'd shown up with a book in hand, prepared to read to him. He had probably hurt her feelings with his lack of interest.

"Reading is a splendid idea," he told her. "What did you bring?"

She darted a quick glance at her elderly cousin. "Cousin Sarah suggested *Pilgrim's Progress.*" She flicked her eyes towards Ben, twisted her mouth, and shrugged. "But perhaps you have a book here that you'd prefer?"

She looked intently at Ben, holding his gaze. But if she was trying to silently communicate something, Ben could not tell what.

"Anything you would like to read would be fine," he said, though he had absolutely no desire to read *Pilgrim's Progress.*

The corners of Lady Wilhelmina's mouth turned down. She must have wanted him to recommend something from his library. But it was too late now, for Aunt Faith bustled off to another room to find a couple of extra chairs. She sat down beside Mrs. Trimmer, leaving Lady Wilhelmina to take the comfortable armchair beside Ben's bed.

Ben fixed what he hoped was a pleasant expression on his face while he listened to the first page of *Pilgrim's Progress.*

Then, to his great relief, his aunt turned to Mrs. Trimmer and said, "Oh, I meant to show you where I plan to put the climbing roses. Do you want to see?"

Mrs. Trimmer glanced doubtfully at Ben, then at her cousin. "Willa, would you like to see the garden, too?" she suggested.

"No, thank you, ma'am. I haven't gotten a chance to read very much yet."

The two older women exchanged Significant Glances. Ben expected one of them to remind Lady Wilhelmina that propriety forbade her staying in a room alone with a gentleman. Reputations could be destroyed by as little as that.

Instead, his aunt smiled and said, "I'm sure Ben will be glad of the company. We won't be gone but a few minutes."

Ben frowned. Did the rules of propriety change when one was sick? Or was Lady Wilhelmina for some reason exempt from them? Middle-aged spinsters could sometimes get away with behavior that would not be tolerated in a debutante, but Lady Wilhelmina looked closer in age to a debutante than a spinster.

Whatever the reason, his aunt and her friend left the room,

talking happily about gardening. In their absence, an uncomfortable silence fell over the room. Ben found himself wishing this were only a nightmare from which he might awaken. But an embarrassing gurgle from his empty stomach made it all too clear that this was no dream.

Maybe he ought to have taken that dose of colic medicine after all. At least then he would have avoided this awkwardness!

Chapter Eight

WILLA WAITED TO speak until she was certain that Cousin Sarah and Miss Marlowe were out of earshot. Then she closed her book with a thump and dropped it carelessly on an empty chair.

"Good." She spoke quietly, not wanting to risk being overheard. "I thought they would never leave!" She reached into her reticule. "Now we can read something more interesting."

Mr. Radcliffe's eyes widened. The poor man looked profoundly confused. Could that be an effect of his illness? Any high fever could cause confusion, in Willa's experience. She saw no tell-tale flush of fever on Mr. Radcliffe's face, but he did look as if he had lost a little weight during his illness.

"I assume you don't really want to listen to *Pilgrim's Progess?*" she asked.

He shook his head. "I'm surprised you brought that. In your first letter, didn't you say you hated that book?"

Willa scrunched up her face. "Hate is too strong a word, but I'm definitely tired of it. I only brought it because I knew Cousin Sarah would approve of it. I have something better to read now that she is out of the way. We got a letter from my uncle yesterday." She pulled the letter out of her bag, unfolded it, and smoothed out the paper.

"You thought I would be entertained by hearing a letter from your uncle?" Mr. Radcliffe looked more confused than ever.

"Not the letter itself," Willa hastened to explain. Though, in fact, Uncle Rowland's letters were often entertaining. "But he writes for the newspaper under a *nom de plume.* He wrote a review of a melodrama he saw at one of the unlicensed theaters, and he sent me a copy. It's quite funny. Would you be interested in hearing it?"

"Of course. That would be lovely."

He did not fool her; she could tell he was only being polite. "It's at least more entertaining than any of the books in Cousin Sarah's house," she promised.

Uncle Rowland's handwriting was not the easiest to read, so Willa had to keep her eyes on the paper. Unable to read the expression on Mr. Radcliffe's face, she did not have any idea how he took the review—not until he laughed out loud halfway through the letter.

"The play couldn't really have been that bad, could it?" he asked.

She glanced up at him then. How his expression had changed listening to the letter! His unexpected smile made his whole face come alive and drew an answering grin from Willa.

"I am afraid I cannot say from experience. I am never allowed to go to this kind of show." Attending a play at Drury Lane or Covent Garden was perfectly acceptable, but Willa's mother believed musical comedies, burlesques, and pantomimes were not suitable for proper young ladies. The rules were different for gentlemen, naturally. "Have you never been yourself?"

Mr. Radcliff shook his head. "I don't care for London."

"Really?" She blinked at him, momentarily at a loss for words. "I thought all young men liked London." She had the impression that most wealthy young gentlemen spent their post-university years in London, getting in fights, falling in love with actresses, and spending too much money.

He scowled. "Not me. It's too smoky, too crowded, too loud, too smelly, too"—he waved a hand in the air as if grasping for words "—too full of people I don't know, whose motives I can't predict. If a gentleman approaches me in the club, I don't know whether he's a new friend or a card sharp looking for his next victim. And if a pretty girl talks to me, I don't know if. . . well, never mind." He flushed a deep red.

Don't know if what? Much as she wondered what Mr. Radcliffe meant, Willa knew she ought not ask. Especially since she was, in fact, a pretty girl.

At least, she hoped he considered her pretty. She probably ought not assume it. Some gentlemen preferred blondes.

"So it's not the city you dislike," Willa suggested, "so much as the people in the city?"

"But that's what makes a city a city!" he pointed out. "It wouldn't be a city if there weren't so many people."

Willa considered that, then shook her head. "It's more complicated than that. Cities have institutions that country villages and market towns often lack. Like the theater." She waved the review in her hand. "Or the opera, or museums."

"I do like museums," Mr. Radcliffe admitted. "But they are best enjoyed on one's own."

"They are?" Willa could not hide her surprise.

"Yes, they are," he said firmly. "If you visit by yourself, when the museum is nearly empty, you can look at the exhibits for as long as you want without worrying that you are slowing anyone down or getting in the way of other parties."

"I suppose so." She remained unconvinced. "I like visiting museums or art galleries with a friend or two, so I can talk about what I see."

If Willa and Phoebe looked at the same painting, they might notice entirely different things about it, while Miss Hadfield's opinions were generally more well-informed. That was part of the fun of visiting an art exhibit. The three of them could have a good conversation together even if they didn't particularly like the exhibit they'd seen.

Mr. Radcliffe frowned. "That only works when you're with

congenial companions, and they are hard to find. But," he added softly, "too easy to lose."

Willa eyed him uncertainly. She heard the pain of some past loss in his voice but could not decide whether she should ask about it. In the end, she held her tongue. Mr. Radcliffe's shuttered expression did not invite such exchanges of confidences.

Instead, she talked about her own "I suppose that is why I have been so unhappy on this trip. My mother and sister cannot keep up with the long rambles I want to take. When they do go out, they generally wish to bathe." She wrinkled her nose, thinking with distaste about the bathing machines on the Newell beach. "I am not convinced of the supposed health benefits of sea-bathing."

"You should have gone somewhere else for a holiday," Mr. Radcliffe concluded. "The lake region, perhaps."

She sighed. "That was what *I* wanted to do, but I was over-ruled. Two against one, you know."

"All the more reason why it is better to take holidays by one-self."

Willa's jaw dropped. "Goodness, you ARE rather a misanthrope, aren't you?" She closed her mouth with an almost audible snap, realizing she'd just said something potentially very rude.

But Mr. Radcliffe did not take offense. "I don't think so." The lines on his forehead grew deeper. "I don't dislike everyone! But as I said earlier, it's difficult to find the right companions. I would be miserable going on holiday with strangers. Going with the right fellow travelers, though, could be better than being alone." He idly picked at the counterpane covering his bed.

Willa rested her chin on her arm as she fumbled through the inchoate idea simmering in her mind. "What traits does a person need in order to be a 'congenial companion' for you?" she wondered aloud.

Mr. Radcliffe ran a hand through his hair, leaving his old-gold curls in disarray. Somehow, this made him look more attractive, rather than less.

"Well, I have to be able to talk to him. Which usually means having common interests. I don't particularly care for social interactions that involve only meaningless pleasantries." He made a face. "I suppose such social graces have their purpose, but. . ." He shrugged. "They do not interest me."

Willa nodded. She doubted that meaningless pleasantries truly interested anyone. That was not their purpose. They existed to lubricate the frictions that could arise between dissimilar people.

Mr. Radcliffe might have less tolerance for idle chatter than most people, but he had been speaking to Willa for a good quarter of an hour, seemingly without boredom. Unless, perhaps, he was good at concealing his disinterest. *Hmm.*

"It is a pity there are no museums nearby," Willa mused out loud. "Or we could experiment."

"Experiment?" He wrinkled his forehead, looking confused.

"To find out whether you could tolerate exploring a museum with me." A hot flush crept up her face as he stared at her, eyes wide. He must think she was frightfully forward! The silence lasted a beat too long before he spoke.

"I don't know of any museums nearby, but there's a shop in Market Caseton that sells fossils. Have you seen it yet?"

Willa shook her head. "I'm afraid neither my mother nor my sister are interested in natural history." Miss Hadfield had more than once talked about looking for fossils, though. She might be convinced to take Willa there.

"When I am over this bout of sickness, I should show you the shop!" Mr. Radcliffe, growing enthusiastic about this plan, leaned closer to her. "It has the largest fossilized ammonite I've ever seen." He held his hands apart to demonstrate. "There are some fascinating fossilized fish, too. And then you could visit the bookseller if you still need reading material."

Eager to accept, Willa opened her mouth—then hesitated, having thought of a potential obstacle. Mr. Radcliffe had probably forgotten that they would need a chaperone whenever they were together. They had only been allowed to talk to each other alone today because Mr. Radcliffe was ill. As it was, she was rather surprised that they had been left alone for so long.

She cleared her throat and tried to raise her objection as tactfully as possible. "I believe we would want to make a party of it, Mr. Radcliffe."

He frowned. "A party? I must say, I don't like large groups of people."

"I understand that," Willa said, "but we could not go there on our own. It would not be proper."

As if they'd been summoned, her cousin and Mr. Radcliffe's aunt appeared in the doorway.

"Go where?" Miss Marlowe asked.

"Lady Wilhelmina and I thought to visit the fossil shop and the bookshop in Caseton. But I suppose she is right that it would not do." Mr. Radcliffe darted an anxious glance at Willa.

Willa smiled reassuringly at him, then lied through her teeth. "I imagine my sister would very much enjoy visiting a fossil shop. If her governess accompanies us, there would be no impropriety. And Phoebe might benefit from a lesson in geology." Never mind the fact that geology bored Phoebe.

"I am afraid Ben will not be going anywhere for the next few days." Miss Marlowe watched him anxiously as she adjusted the pillows supporting him. "He has been quite unwell these last few days, you know."

Her nephew made a moue of distaste. "I am perfectly well now! It was just an upset stomach, Aunt Faith. It is not as if I were on the verge of dying!"

Cousin Sarah smoothly intervened before aunt and nephew could start quarrelling. "Well, you must send us a note when you do feel up to an excursion, Mr. Radcliffe. It sounds like something the young people would enjoy, and I am sure that Miss Hadfield would not mind accompanying them."

"A lovely plan, *when Ben is up to it.*" A stern look from Miss Marlowe underscored the second half of the sentence.

Mr. Radcliffe's face fell, but he made no protest. "It was good of you to call on me, Mrs. Trimmer, Lady Wilhelmina." He looked beseechingly at Willa, but she had no idea what he sought from her.

Cousin Sarah caught Willa's eye and subtly turned her head towards the door. It was time to go.

"We hope to find you in better health when next we see you, Mr. Radcliffe," Cousin Sarah said.

Willa murmured her agreement and followed the older woman out of the room, still wondering what that last look from Mr. Radcliffe meant. Maybe he'd been trying to convey some concern about the proposed outing—something he did not want to discuss in front of his aunt. But she had no idea what that might be. How unfortunate that young ladies and gentlemen were so rarely allowed to converse alone! It made open communication quite difficult.

Her mind full of unanswerable questions, Willa remained silent all the way home.

Chapter Nine

May, 1822

"S O TELL ME, who exactly is this Lady Willow-whatever that we're going to meet?" Marlowe Millington sprawled across the forward-facing carriage seat, taking up far more than his fair share of space. A lock of dark hair fell in front of his eyes, and he pushed it back with what looked like a practiced gesture.

Ben, sitting rigidly upright, faced his cousin from the opposite side of the barouche. A combination of irritation and anxiety kept him tense all the way from the tower to Mrs. Trimmer's house, where they were to meet the Selwyn ladies.

"Lady Wilhelmina and Lady Phoebe are the daughters of the late Earl of Inglewhite. They were ill this winter and have come to Newell for their health." Irritation grated in Ben's voice. This was hardly the first time he'd explained that to Marlowe.

Marlowe was probably trying to ask a different question entirely, but Ben was not in the mood to play guessing games. If there were something Marlowe wanted to know, he should speak more plainly.

"But how did *you* come to know them? Pardon my saying, but I hadn't thought *you* were in the petticoat line." Marlowe might have intended his expression to be a smile, but it looked more like a sneer.

Ben rolled his eyes and stared out over the side of the open carriage. Sunbeams danced in and out of shadows cast by the fluffy clouds overhead. Birds sang their most enthusiastic spring songs, and the breeze was just brisk enough to waft the briny odor of the ocean inland. Such a shame that this lovely spring day had to be shared with one of his most annoying relatives.

But it would be rude not to answer Marlowe's question. "I fell into conversation with Lady Wilhelmina by purest happenstance, and we discovered we had some mutual interests." Ben saw no need to explain that at one point, he'd assumed he was corresponding with a "William" rather than "Wilhelmina." He still inwardly cringed whenever he thought of that.

By now, he'd gotten past his initial disappointment. Lady Wilhelmina's gender created complications for their friendship (i.e. the need for chaperones), but Ben had begun to hope her being a girl was not the insurmountable barrier he'd originally feared it would be.

Marlowe, on the other hand, might be a real obstacle. Bad enough that he showed up unannounced yesterday. Today he'd invited himself along on the outing to Caseton. Worst of all, he'd brought a whole trunk with him and had spoken of staying on at the Tower during the summer season, meaning he might be planning on sticking around for months.

Ben's scowl deepened as he contemplated that dreadful possibility. The only person who seemed happy to see Marlowe had been Ben's grandfather. As Joseph Marlowe's oldest grandson, Marlowe had long been assumed to be the future owner of Marlowe Tower. Ben, who would inherit his father's comfortable estate and a baronet's title, did not begrudge his cousins any of the Marlowe family wealth. But he did wonder why his grandfather had singled out *Marlowe*, of all the Millington children. Normally, Grandfather had better taste!

The carriage slowed to a stop, and Marlowe reached across the footwell to tap Ben's knee. Ben glared at him. His cousin knew he didn't like unexpected touches! At least, he ought to know that by now.

Marlowe turned to look at Mrs. Trimmer's handsome stone

house, and his mouth fell ajar. "I say, Ben, do you mean to tell me that *that* pretty girl is your friend?" he whispered.

Ben turned to look too. Sure enough, Miss Hadfield and the Selwyn sisters spilled out of the house into the front garden, armed with bonnets, reticules, and parasols. Mrs. Trimmer followed them out, waving cheerfully.

"You're going to have to move over to make room," Ben hissed. Fitting five people into a carriage meant to seat only four was already going to be a challenge, and Marlowe's outstretched limbs would make it even harder.

He need not have worried. Though Marlowe saw no need to show respect to his younger cousin, the Selwyn ladies received quite different treatment. Marlowe lifted his hat and bowed to them. "Good morning, ladies. I hope you do not mind me tagging along on your outing. I am delighted to meet any friends of Ben's."

Miss Hadfield glanced at Ben, raising her brows in inquiry.

Ben set his irritation aside to make the necessary introductions. "Lady Wilhelmina, Lady Phoebe, Miss Hadfield? May I introduce my cousin, Marlowe Millingford? He is visiting from Winchester." Ben would like to have apologized for Marlowe's unwanted presence, but he could think of no way to do that without offending his cousin.

"Pleased to meet you, Mr. Millingford." Despite her perfunctory smile, Miss Hadfield looked concerned rather than pleased.

But the two Selwyn sisters smiled, nodded, and murmured soft greetings. If they were unhappy about having a stranger tag along with them, they concealed their feelings well.

Of course, they had no way of knowing how obnoxious Marlowe was.

Miss Hadfield took charge of the seating problem. "Mr. Radcliffe, if you sit next to your cousin, I believe the three of us can squeeze together on one seat. We will all be quite cozy."

"An excellent plan!" Ben ought to have thought of that himself. Rather, Marlowe ought to have moved to make room.

"Marlowe, will you join me, so the ladies may have the forward-facing seat?" Ben hated facing backward as much as anyone, but courtesy required gentlemen to give the preferred seat to the ladies.

"Ah, yes." Marlowe smiled winningly at Miss Hadfield as he settled next to Ben. "I very much appreciate your kindness in letting me accompany you to Caseton today. Otherwise, I'd be rambling around the tower with nothing to do but play backgammon with my grandfather."

"There's nothing wrong with backgammon," Ben protested. Besides, he doubted that Marlowe had ever played backgammon with Grandfather Marlowe. Marlowe's youngest sister often played it when she visited, but Ben had never seen Marlowe doing so.

"Yes, I used to love playing it with our great-aunt." Lady Phoebe smiled brightly for a moment, and then her smile faded. "Unfortunately, Aunt Agatha passed away a few years ago. I don't believe I've played backgammon since."

"If you ever visit Marlowe Tower, I'm sure my grandfather would oblige you with a game," Ben told her.

Ben only meant to console the child, but when her eyes widened with surprise, he worried that he'd said the wrong thing. He darted a glance at Miss Hadfield, half-expecting to see the sort of stern look he'd often received from his tutor. But Miss Hadfield's face showed no sign of irritation or surprise, so he allowed himself to relax.

By the time the carriage reached the nearby market town, Ben reluctantly admitted to himself that Marlowe's presence had been a blessing in disguise. Whereas Ben struggled to think of appropriate things to discuss, Marlowe had a gift for conversation. Some might even call him charming—though Ben disagreed. He still remembered the many times his cousin had mocked or bullied him over the years.

What bothered Ben most was the way Lady Wilhelmina replied to Marlowe. She brushed aside Marlowe's few attempts at gallantry, but she met his humorous remarks with witticisms of her own. She did not laugh out loud as often as her younger sister did, but she smiled frequently.

Too frequently. It was unfair that a man as cruel and selfish as Marlowe Millington could make a favorable impression on such a pleasant young woman.

Ben sat in silence, unable to find a way to join the conversation, until Marlowe decided to tease him. "What are you glowering at, Benji? You look like you have a stomachache!"

Lady Wilhelmina turned toward Ben, her eyes soft with concern. "I hope you are not still sick! I would not have agreed to this excursion if I thought you were unwell. I should feel terrible if you suffered a relapse because we dragged you with us."

"I am not the least bit sick," Ben assured her. "And no one had to drag me along today."

"You must excuse my cousin," Marlowe said. "Being tongue-tied is quite his usual state. I'm afraid he inherited our grandfather's taciturn disposition. We ought not expect more than a handful of words from him today."

To a stranger, Marlowe's grin might have looked playful, but Ben recognized it for the mockery it really was. He tightened his jaw and clenched his hands into fists. This was precisely why he hadn't wanted his cousin to join their party.

"Really?" Lady Wilhelmina raised her brows, turning her friendliness into hauteur. A hint of chill entered her voice as she told Marlowe, "I have heard Mr. Radcliffe speak quite eloquently on subjects that interest him." She turned back to Ben. "Have you found any noteworthy pieces of sea glass recently?"

A tight knot at the center of Ben's chest loosened. Lady Wilhelmina had just given him an entrance into the conversation. And she had spoken to him with far more warmth than she showed Marlowe.

Not that her reaction mattered, of course. It was not as if the two cousins were competing for her attention.

"No new sea glass," he informed her, "but I did find a scrap of pottery. That's much rarer than glass, at least around here."

He opened his mouth to tell her about his jewelry-making plans, then hesitated. Would it not be better to keep that a surprise? Especially since propriety forbade a gentleman from giving gifts to a young lady, unless they were betrothed. Ben was most certainly not betrothed to Lady Wilhelmina, and he didn't want to be.

Did he? For a startling moment, his heart seemed to stop. Why wouldn't he want to marry Lady Wilhelmina? She was beautiful, intelligent, and well-mannered. When Ben inherited his father's title and estate, he might benefit from having a wife who could help him navigate social settings.

But he was getting ahead of himself. An earl's daughter might very well intend to marry into the peerage. She and her family might not consider a future baronet as an eligible suitor. It was presumptuous of Ben to assume Lady Wilhelmina might encourage his suit.

"Lord, Ben, your wits have gone wandering again! What are you dreaming about now?" Marlowe chuckled to take the bite out of his words.

Heat flushed Ben's face. "Sorry, I became distracted." He snapped his mouth shut and tightened his lips.

He would like to have continued exploring the startling possibility of pursuing a courtship rather than friendship with Lady Wilhelmina, but he did not foresee many quiet moments of reflection occurring in the next few hours. He would have to think about it later.

"Is this the shop that sells fossils?" Miss Hadfield asked.

Ben forced himself to pay attention to his surroundings again. "Ah, yes. Bartlett's started off as a curiosity shop, but it has a large collection of fossils. Bartlett sells sea glass, agates, and other such souvenirs, too."

The shopkeeper also repaired jewelry. If Ben had been here alone, he might have asked if Bartlett knew anything about making jewelry from sea glass. He was not likely to have the opportunity today, unless he found some way to separate himself from the rest of the party. Could he come up with some pretext for running back to the shop while the others were at the bakery or bookshop?

Lady Wilhelmina's musical speaking voice broke through Ben's woolgathering. "Why, thank you, Mr. Millington."

Ben immediately swiveled his head around, curious about what Marlowe had done to win Lady Wilhelmina's gratitude. His heart sank. While Ben had been lost in his own head, Marlowe had stepped out of the barouche and was now helping the Selwyn sisters out of the carriage.

Marlowe caught Ben's eye, and one side of his mouth curled up in a smug smile. "It's nothing, my lady," he suavely replied. "Any gentleman would have extended the same courtesy—assuming he was awake enough to notice when his help was needed."

Ben glared at his cousin, but he could hardly argue with him. Ben ought to have thought of helping the ladies. Losing the chance to display his courtesy left him feeling like he'd lost a hand at a card game.

Of course, this was real life, not a game. There weren't winners and losers. *Right?*

When Marlowe gallantly offered Lady Wilhelmina his arm to escort her into the curiosity shop, Ben revised his opinion. It looked as if Marlowe was playing to win. When they were children, Marlowe usually *had* won when it came to games of strength or agility. Ben lacked his cousin's athletic ability.

On the other hand, when it came to games of strategy, Ben generally triumphed. Marlowe did not have the patience for a long game of chess. Nor did he possess Ben's knowledge of fossils, seashells, and other treasures found on the beach.

When it came down to it, Ben really held the trump card in this round, didn't he? At least for this part of the outing—and maybe for the visit to the bookshop, too. Marlowe had never been much of a reader. Ben squared his shoulders, offered his arm to Miss Hadfield, and picked up the hand he'd been dealt.

Chapter Ten

IF THERE WAS anything better than capturing the attention of one handsome young man, it would be having a second beau. At least, other young ladies seemed to think so. Last year, Willa had been fascinated by the way the Season's diamonds held court, distributing smiles and attention to one gallant one day and another the next, as if it were an amusing game.

To Willa, those flirtation games had seemed like a waste of everyone's time. They still seemed so now. She found nothing amusing about the tension between Mr. Radcliffe and his uninvited cousin.

Mr. Millington initially appeared charming, even suave— quite unlike shy, nervous Mr. Radcliffe. Willa was surprised by the way Mr. Radcliffe glared at Mr. Millington. Weren't they cousins?

But as she listened more carefully, she detected cruel undercurrents to Mr. Millington's conversation. His words were not necessarily offensive in themselves, but the taunting tone with which he uttered them grew stronger as the afternoon wore on.

In the curiosity shop, Mr. Radcliffe could easily match his more dashing cousin. He identified seashells at Phoebe's request, found some curious rock samples that delighted Miss Hadfield, and somehow pulled a beautiful purple gem out of a box containing mostly blue and white sea glass. By the time they left the curiosity shop laden with souvenirs, Mr. Radcliffe walked with a more confident spring to his step. A smile lingered on Willa's face at the sight.

Her smile fell when Mr. Radcliffe's cousin got his revenge at the bakery. Phoebe announced that she was hungry, so Mr. Millington suggested stopping at the baker's shop around the corner.

"This place is famous for their fairy cakes," he explained. Phoebe's eyes immediately brightened.

"They usually sell out of fairy cakes quickly," Mr. Radcliffe warned. "At this hour, we will be lucky to find any kind of sweet buns for tea."

"Oh, I hope they have fairy cakes! Those are my favorite." Phoebe galloped at a most unladylike pace towards the shop, leaving Miss Hadfield and Willa trailing after her.

Miss Hadfield snorted. Willa caught her eye, and they exchanged a wry smile. Both of them tried to step faster without appearing to run.

"Evidently we need to devote more time to our deportment lessons," Miss Hadfield murmured.

"There is only so much deportment lessons can accomplish," Willa warned. Running down the street in search of cake might be undignified behavior, but it was very Phoebe.

By the time the rest of the party reached the bakery, Phoebe had discovered that there were indeed no fairy cakes left on display. She lamented the situation at length, though fortunately not very loudly.

While Phoebe complained, Mr. Millington began to whisper to the woman behind the counter.

"Phoebe," Miss Hadfield said, "a lady does not lose her composure over something as trivial as being deprived of a preferred treat. There are hungry children in Ireland who would be happy to eat anything—"

"I know," Phoebe interjected, "but the gentlemen got my hopes up talking about fairy cakes." She sent a reproachful look over her shoulder at Mr. Radcliffe.

"I am very sorry about that," Mr. Radcliffe replied. "But you know, the currant buns here are quite good. Can you make do with that?"

"I suppose that's better than cabbage soup," Phoebe agreed.

The mention of cabbages momentarily confused Willa. By the time she worked out that it was a reference to the hungry children in Ireland, Phoebe had turned back to the counter and was asking for currant buns.

"Wouldn't you rather have the fairy cakes, Lady Phoebe?" Everyone turned to stare at Mr. Millington, who grinned broadly. "Mrs. Crofts just sold me the last ones."

"I was saving 'em for my grandchildren," explained the woman behind the counter, "but this young gentleman convinced me to sell them instead."

Phoebe's eyes widened. "Oh, thank you Mr. Millington! And thank you, ma'am." She beamed as Mrs. Crofts handed Mr. Millington a plate laden with fairy cakes and currant buns.

"I'll fetch your tea in half a minute," Mrs. Crofts promised.

Though the counter full of bread, cakes, and other baked goods took up most of one wall, there was room on the other side of the shop for a few small tables and chairs. Willa led Phoebe to one of the tables, assuming that Miss Hadfield would follow them. To her dismay, Mr. Millington took the last seat, forcing Miss Hadfield and Mr. Radcliffe to sit at a different table.

Willa knew Haddy wouldn't mind that—she seemed disposed to like Mr. Radcliffe. But Willa minded it! She would rather have had Mr. Radcliffe at her table. To be sure, Mr. Millington had good conversation. He kept Willa and Phoebe well entertained throughout their tea. But Willa had agreed to this outing because she wished for Mr. Radcliffe's company, not his cousin's.

Besides, Willa had the uncomfortable feeling that Mr. Millington was trying too hard to charm her. He mentioned something about the Lake poets, but when Willa admitted that she preferred novels over poetry, he avowed a deep fondness for the works of Sir Walter Scott.

Before Willa had time to get too irritated, Miss Hadfield rose from her chair and interrupted their conversation. "Wilhelmina, if you wish to visit the bookseller, we had better go now, before the afternoon gets much later. We would not want to be late for dinner."

"Oh, yes! I do want to visit the book shop." True as that was, Willa's smile owed more to her relief at no longer being stuck at a table with Mr. Millington.

As the group wended their way down the street, Phoebe began whining again. "Can't we just go home?" she begged. "I am too tired to keep wandering around town."

"It's a pity that I haven't got my gig with me," Mr. Millington said. "It would be ideal for navigating these narrow streets."

The streets were no narrower than those of other market towns, so far as Willa could tell. Mr. Millington merely wanted to brag about his horse and carriage. The smile he directed at her now might look friendly, but having seen how Mr. Millington sneered at his cousin, Willa had tired of his charm.

It didn't hurt that Mr. Radcliffe, with his golden hair and striking green eyes, was better looking than Mr. Millington.

"Only if you can control your horse better than you did the last time you were here," Mr. Radcliffe retorted. "I seem to recall you crashing into a fence post on your way into town."

The look Mr. Millington gave his cousin could have frozen over a hot spring. "That was not my doing! It was the fault of that blasted nag I used to own. My new horse has a much softer mouth."

Mr. Radcliffe opened his mouth, looking as if he meant to argue further, but Willa intervened before the conversation could grow more heated. "Is this the bookshop you patronize?" she asked. "How charming!"

She did not exaggerate: The shop *was* charming. Thatcher's Stationery occupied the corner of a long building. The plate-glass window displayed open folios, artful bookends, and elegant inkstands.

"Ah, yes, this is the best stationer's shop in the county, and the only place you can find a tolerable selection of books." Mr. Radcliffe scored a point on his cousin by holding the door open for the ladies.

Maybe that was why Mr. Millington scowled as he strolled into the shop. Or maybe he did not really care for reading. He did not seem particularly interested in any of the books on display.

Willa, on the other hand, pounced when she saw a familiar name in gilt lettering. "Oh, you stock Mr. Kirkland's books! Do you have the new one?" She held her breath as she waited, hardly daring to hope.

"You mean *Terror at Carringford Park?*" The bookseller gave a regretful shake of her head. "We did have it, but we only had a few copies, and someone bought the very last one yesterday. We have a copy for our circulating library, but the waiting list is already half a page long. I would be happy to order a copy for you, though, miss."

Willa's shoulders slumped. She had expected as much, but it was still a disappointment. "No need to order it, ma'am. I am sure I will have a chance to buy it later." If worse came to worst, she would ask Uncle Rowland to send her a copy. He generally knew where to find the most fashionable books.

Mr. Radcliffe peered over Willa's shoulder, studying the copy of *Midnight Secrets* on display. "G.W. Kirkland? I don't recognize that name. What does he write?"

Willa paused to figure out how best to characterize Kirkland's work. "They are stories in the Gothic line, I suppose, but more like the *The Mysteries of Udolpho* than like *The Castle of Otranto* or Beckford's *The Monk*. Kirkland's plots are full of secrets and mysteries, but they never contain supernatural events. His first book was about Recusants."

Mr. Millington grimaced. "I prefer books with some excitement in them, like *The Monk*. Recusants sound like something out of a history lesson, don't you think?" He smiled perfunctorily before walking away to look at a display of printed murder trials.

He *would* like a book like *The Monk*! Willa thought scornfully. She turned away from him to study one of Sir Walter Scott's recent novels. Hadn't *The Monk* been John Thorpe's favorite book in *Northanger Abbey*? She looked back over her shoulder at Mr. Millington, wondering if he played the part of John Thorpe in her story. If so, did that make Mr. Radcliffe a stand-in for Henry Tilney?

She stole a quick glance at Mr. Radcliffe, who was now deep in conversation with the shopkeeper. In personality, Benjamin Radcliffe did not resemble any of the heroes of Miss Austen's novels. Nor did Willa herself share much with the foolish, overly imaginative Catherine Morland. At least, she hoped not!

But. . . did she want the same thing of Mr. Radcliffe that Catherine Morland had wanted of Henry Tilney? Merely asking herself the question unsettled Willa. When she tossed the bottle into the ocean a few weeks ago, she'd hoped for nothing more than a friendship that might alleviate the months of boredom ahead. Surely, that hadn't changed.

"I believe I will take this book," Willa told the shopkeeper. *The Pirate* might not be as thrilling as the newest G.W. Kirkland book, but it had to be more entertaining than the late Mr. Trimmer's collection of sermons.

As Willa walked out of the shop with her purchase tucked under her arm, she wondered how she would even know if her feelings for Mr. Radcliffe had changed. She knew what it was like to fancy a young man from afar, or to enjoy a light flirtation with a gentleman who intended nothing more than amusement. But she had no idea what it might be like to go from friendship to romantic love.

There must be some kind of sign when one's feelings changed. But although she had been advised on how to tell if a gentleman was interested in her, she had never been taught how to evaluate her own feelings or desires.

Maybe Mama could explain it. Willa resolved to ask when she got back home.

"Mr. Radcliffe," Phoebe chirped, "what book did you buy?"

Willa glanced up at him, surprised. She hadn't realized he'd bought a book at all. Even more surprisingly, the tops of his ears turned red with embarrassment.

"Oh, um. Well, I thought I should try one of Mr. Kirkland's novels. I bought the first one, *Midnight Secrets*." His blush deepened when he caught her eye.

A jolt of pure delight made Willa's heart skip a beat. Mr. Radcliffe had gotten the book because *she* liked Kirkland's novels. She was certain of it.

"You'll have to tell me how you like it." She looked steadily ahead at the waiting carriage, certain that anyone who caught her eye would see her excitement.

Of course, him buying a book because Willa liked the author did not mean he was sweet on her, Willa reminded herself. Friends often recommended books to each other. Half the fun of a good book came from talking about it afterward. Hadn't that been one of the things she'd hoped to find when she sent her message out into the world? She was lucky to have found a friend here in Dorsetshire, and she ought not expect more than friendship from Mr. Radcliffe.

He did look rather sweet when he blushed, though.

On the way home, the lively good cheer from the start of the outing faded. People were tired and, at least in Phoebe's case, cranky. Mr. Radcliffe disappeared behind the pages of his book. Willa, pleased to at last have an interesting new book to read, needed no urging to do the same.

At first, she worried that Miss Hadfield would scold her for being unsociable. But Haddy, who had closed her eyes, looked to be on the verge of falling asleep. If Haddy were ill-disposed for conversation herself, she was unlikely to scold Willa for reading instead of conversing with others.

After a few failed attempts to engage people in conversation, Mr. Millington opted to read, too. Instead of a novel, he'd bought an account of a woman tried for poisoning her husband. It seemed like morbid reading to Willa, but at least it held his attention, thereby preventing him from bothering her.

Her own book seemed promising, but by the time the barouche finally rolled up to Cousin Sarah's house, Willa felt half-asleep. She must not have been the only one—Phoebe unsuccessfully tried to smother a yawn.

Willa caught Mr. Radcliffe's eye and smiled ruefully. "It has been a rather long day, hasn't it?"

"A very pleasant one, though. We are most grateful to you for accompanying us, Mr. Radcliffe, Mr. Millington." Miss Hadfield nodded briskly at the gentlemen, then urged Phoebe to gather up her things.

"Yes, thank you very much." It was probably rude of her, but Willa ignored Mr. Millington as she bestowed a grateful smile upon Mr. Radcliffe.

He returned the gesture with a sweet, uncertain smile of his own. "It was my pleasure. Perhaps"—he darted a glance at his cousin, who had put his book down to listen—"I am sure I will see you about, Lady Wilhelmina."

Willa felt a flicker of disappointment; for a moment, she'd thought he meant to suggest a future meeting. But Mr. Radcliffe caught her eye and shook his head fractionally, and she realized that, whatever he'd been about to say, he did not want to say it in front of Mr. Millington. Interesting.

"Yes, I am sure we will see each other soon," Willa agreed. She let Mr. Millington help her out of the carriage but paid him little notice aside from a nod of thanks. She did not want to encourage his attentions.

Once they were inside, Miss Hadfield handed her bonnet to the waiting servant, then turned towards Willa. "I think that went very well, despite a certain visitor tagging along when he wasn't wanted. But I daresay the presence of a rival may have a salutary effect on Mr. Radcliffe."

Willa narrowed her eyes as she studied her former governess. "What do you mean, a salutary effect?"

The corners of Miss Hadfield's mouth lifted, giving her a distinctly smug expression. "Sometimes an admirer needs the sting of competition to move him to action. Much like the way some racehorses run faster when surrounded by competitors, you know."

Willa's heart pattered unevenly. "I don't know that Mr. Radcliffe admires me in that way," she cautioned. "Maybe he only wanted to show us around because he knew we were unfamiliar with Market Caseton. He might only have meant to be neighborly."

Miss Hadfield snorted. "Do you think he would put up with his cousin's insults for an entire afternoon out of disinterested kindness? Because I do not. I daresay he feels more than *neighborly* towards you, my dear. Watch him closely next time if you do not believe me."

Willa tried to ignore the blush she felt rising on her face. "We shall see," she said, unwilling to commit to more. She had no idea when she would have another chance to observe Mr. Radcliffe.

Chapter Eleven

B EN RESOLVED TO wait until Marlowe returned to Hampshire before seeking out Lady Wilhelmina again. He did not want to endure another afternoon of Marlowe's sneers and jibes. And he would rather have Lady Wilhelmina's company all to himself.

How anyone could pursue a courtship surrounded by watchful guardians and chaperones mystified Ben. Since the relationship between husband and wife was both intimate and permanent, one would think prospective spouses should spend a good deal of time together before binding themselves in matrimony. Instead, propriety made meeting alone with a respectable young lady nearly impossible.

Aside from that, Ben wanted his cousin gone for other reasons. During his unwanted visit, Marlowe knocked over Ben's jar of peppermints, spilling the candy Aunt Patience had made all over the floor.

Marlowe also scattered a box of seashells across the counter. Ben ejected Marlowe from his workshop, but the damage had been done. He had to throw out all the candy, and some of the shells were chipped or cracked.

Things didn't go much better in the house itself. For nearly a week, Marlowe followed Aunt Faith around, asking impertinent questions about everyone's health and eating habits. He barged in on Grandfather Marlowe, waking him from naps and disturbing him while at work—rather a risky choice, if he wanted to keep Grandfather's favor.

"Grandfather certainly seems to be feeling his age these days," Marlowe observed to Ben. "His temper is much worse."

"That's only because you interrupted him when he was writing," Ben explained. "The editor of *The Current Review* asked him to write a response to someone's criticism of Alexander Pope. He's been working on that for weeks. Surely you know he never likes being interrupted while writing." Or when he was reading, for that matter.

"Oh, Alexander Pope," Marlowe scoffed. "I didn't think anyone read that stuff anymore! The work of modern poets is much more natural. I quite side with Mr. Hunt on that point."

"I would avoid saying that where Grandfather can hear you," Ben warned. "He may be a little hard of hearing, but he doesn't miss much. And he can still out-argue a lawyer." He shuddered, remembering some of the convoluted arguments he'd had with his grandfather since moving to Marlowe Tower.

"Still, don't you think his health is waning?" Marlowe pushed. "What about this dyspepsia? He seems to suffer it quite often."

Ben shrugged. Aunt Faith thought Grandfather's dyspepsia was nothing more than his body rebelling against too rich a diet. But he did not want to explain that to Marlowe. What business was it of his what Grandfather could or couldn't eat?

He limited himself to saying, "His health seems as good now as it was when I moved into the Tower, and that was over a year ago." Had he really been here that long? "He hasn't had one of his chest colds in months."

"When he writes to my mother, he always complains of ill-health," Marlowe said. "Mother was a little worried."

"Oh, that." Ben smiled. "Yes, he does like to complain. And it is true that he has many of the complaints one would expect of a man his age—arthritis, bad teeth, and so on. But I assure you, his physician is quite pleased with his progress. You may tell your mother there is no cause for concern."

Marlowe stared at Ben, an odd expression on his face. "That is good news." He sounded unconvinced, but he dropped the argument.

Fortunately, all bad things come to an end, and Marlowe finally left Dorset, returning to Winchester and his work. As soon as Marlowe's carriage disappeared around the first curve in the road, Ben dashed off a note to Lady Wilhelmina, inviting her to go for a ride with him as soon as the weather allowed.

She returned the note with an acceptance but requested that Miss Hadfield accompany them.

Miss Hadfield is an experienced equestrienne, but rarely gets the chance to ride these days, since my sister does not care for horse exercise. If you can loan her a suitable mount, we would be most appreciative.

Ben did not, for one minute, think that Miss Hadfield wanted to accompany them purely out of a fondness for horses. She would be present to chaperone Lady Wilhelmina. As if Ben were going to do what, exactly? Persuade Lady Wilhelmina to gallop off to Gretna Green with him? Rather a long way to ride on horseback!

And probably unnecessary, he thought more seriously. Given the friendly reception he'd received from Lady Wilhelmina's family, Ben had no reason to think they would disapprove of his suit. Assuming that he did intend to court Lady Wilhelmina, which he had not yet decided.

But if Ben met with Lady Wilhelmina to go riding together, wouldn't people assume he was already courting her? This was exactly why Ben usually tried to avoid interacting with women; he never knew how much or how little attention would be taken as a sign of interest.

Ben shook his head, but his concerns did not stop him from sealing his reply and sending it back with the servant who had brought Lady Wilhelmina's message. This time, he was willing to risk the possibility of an entanglement.

WHEN LADY WILHELMINA showed up for the scheduled ride, she arrived without her chaperone.

Ben stared blankly at her, but before he could inquire after her companion, she explained. "Miss Hadfield had to stay behind on account of a cold. My mother said I could ride with you anyway, so long as we had a groom accompanying us for the sake of propriety."

"Splendid!" Ben said and meant it.

Ben often had trouble following the conversation in a group setting. Having only one person to talk to would make things easier. He would only have to evaluate one person's reactions, too, rather than trying to watch two people's faces to see if he'd somehow blundered.

Timothy, the groom who accompanied Ben and his guest, trailed so far behind the two young people that they might as well have been alone. Things couldn't have fallen out more perfectly.

Ben and Lady Wilhelmina talked about horses, riding, and driving. Ben knew how to drive a one-horse carriage, but had never driven a pair or team, while Lady Wilhelmina had never learned to drive at all.

"Is it harder than riding?" she asked.

Ben frowned as he considered that. "Not harder, but different. You don't have to worry about your seat, but you do have to be aware of how much space there is in the road. If you miscalculate, someone might get hurt." He had run his tilbury into a hedge once or twice, but at least he'd never crashed into another vehicle.

"It sounds like fun." She must have realized how wistful she sounded. "Of course, riding is a good deal of fun, too. I am lucky to have learned that. Many girls don't ride at all."

"If you wanted," Ben said hesitantly, "I could teach you how to drive. Although I suppose we'd have to have a groom with us, for propriety's sake."

She grimaced. "Propriety be damned!" She glanced back over her shoulder at the groom.

Ben looked, too, but saw nothing to worry about. If Timothy had overheard, his impassive face showed no reaction. Ben turned back to Lady Wilhelmina and smiled. "You must get rather tired of having to worry about your reputation all the time."

"I most certainly do." She spoke softly, but fiercely. "Being a young lady means no one ever trusts you to do anything on your own."

"Is it *you* they don't trust, or the people around you?" Ben wondered.

Her mouth twisted into a crooked smile. "Probably both. Which seems ridiculous, doesn't it? It isn't as if all men are wolves waiting for a chance to swallow an innocent lamb whole."

"I don't think wolves *can* swallow a lamb whole," Ben argued. "A chick, maybe, or a baby rabbit, even, but—"

Lady Wilhelmina laughed. "I did not mean it so literally."

"Of course not." Ben's face burned with shame. He knew that! The metaphor of wolves preying on sheep was such a common one that there was no excuse for his pedantry. "I suppose I agree with you. For the most part."

On the other hand. . . he frowned as he remembered scraps of vulgar conversation he'd overheard at school. "Men can be quite lecherous," he warned. "Even gentlemen." He'd seen some of that behavior firsthand at Cambridge.

"No doubt," she agreed, "but I know many men who are upright and decent, even when they think no one is watching. I'm certain that my Uncle Richard, for example, has never been anything but a gentleman." She glanced askance at him. "I don't for one moment believe that *you* would behave badly towards a woman, Mr. Radcliffe. I am sure you could be trusted alone with a lady."

Ben looked away, lest she read his mixed feelings. On the one hand, he hoped he would never be predatory in his treatment of women, whether they were of his own class or of the lower orders.

On the other hand, he *was* a man. He admired an attractive woman as much as anyone else. In fact, he admired Lady Wilhelmina a great deal. He would have liked to do more than admire, if the situation allowed it. For instance, a loose strand of hair had escaped from underneath her riding hat, and he longed to tuck it behind her ear, maybe letting his fingertips linger on her cheek. . .

But the situation most certainly did *not* allow that. He could not even tell her how much he wished he could touch her, how much he wondered if her skin was as soft as it looked. . .

"Do you have any beaus?" he blurted out.

"Do I have any *what*?" Her eyes widened.

"I just thought a young lady like you would have, you know, suitors. Admirers. Or something." That tell-tale blush burned on his cheekbones again. "My apologies, my lady. It was an impertinent question. Please forget I said anything."

Instead of taking offense, she answered him. "I do not have a beau, Mr. Radcliffe. I had a few suitors during my first Season, but none of them. . . well, there were none whom I cared for well enough to entertain an offer."

Ben hoped she could not see the relief on his face. "I suppose it must be hard to get to know people during a London Season."

"Have you never been to London during the Season?" The surprise in her voice brought his eyes back to her face.

"Me?" He chuckled somewhat bitterly. "Indeed not! Remember, I do not like London, and I would like *tonnish* events even less. I do not care for noisy parties, houses filled to bursting, or having to exchange idle chatter with strangers." He fought the urge to shudder at the wave of revulsion that swept over him. "I attended the Bath season for a few weeks last year, but I did not care for that, either."

Grandfather Marlowe might have enjoyed exchanging reminiscences with other elderly men, but there was little to entertain Ben in either the Pump Room or the Assembly Rooms. Besides, the water from the hot springs tasted terrible. He refused to believe it had any medicinal properties.

"I don't mind large crushes, but I prefer country parties myself," Lady Wilhelmina admitted. "At a small country dance, one is sure to likely to know most of the guests, which is not true in London or Bath."

"Yes, I quite agree." He hoped that meant Lady Wilhelmina would not expect her future husband to spend the Season with her in London every year. Not that that mattered to Ben, of course. It wasn't as if he had decided to offer for her.

All the same, her answer relieved Ben. Even the profoundest romantic love couldn't transform an oddity like Ben into one of the sprigs of fashion who flourished in *tonnish* drawing rooms.

Chapter Twelve

I T WAS A pleasant ride, except for all the undercurrents in the conversation. Sometimes Willa thought she imagined them. Other times, the sight of a bashful or thoughtful expression on Mr. Radcliffe's face convinced her that both she and Mr. Radcliff contemplated sentiments they were not yet ready to share.

Not that *Willa* could have said anything, even if she had known what she wanted to say. That would be unladylike. Unless Mr. Radcliffe brought up the subject of matrimony, she could not say anything about it—no matter how much she might wish she could turn to him and ask, "Do you view me purely as a friend or as a potential wife?"

She would not have been heartbroken if all he wanted was friendship, but she wanted to *know*. It was hard to know how to interact with him when she did not know what he wanted.

All the uncertainties disturbed Willa so much, she blurted out something she would normally have kept to herself. Their ride took them on a loop around the park, and the gravel trail ran alongside the edge of the cliffs overlooking the sea. Mr. Radcliffe suggested they dismount so they could get a better look. The groom held their mounts, leaving them free to explore on foot.

Willa's heart beat faster as she approached the edge of the cliff. She had hoped to avoid going anywhere near the water. The ocean was much rougher here than at the cove. There was no lovely strip of sand below: only rocks and the angry, whitecapped breakers crashing over them. The wind blew the briny scent of the ocean straight into Willa's face, making her stomach churn.

Beyond the breakers, the ocean spread all the way to the horizon: dark, unknowable, deadly. Every muscle in Willa's body tensed at the sight of it. Normally, she avoided staring out over such seascapes, but they had stopped here to admire the view. It would seem decidedly odd if she refused to look at the ocean at all. She clenched her jaw and prayed that they did not linger here long enough for her to get a headache.

Politeness demanded a positive response to the panorama spread before her, so Willa did her best to hide her anxiety. "This is a lovely view." That felt like a safe compliment. She might wish herself elsewhere, but she knew most people would consider the view beautiful rather than dreadful.

"I have always thought being so close to the ocean was the best thing about Marlowe Tower," Mr. Radcliffe confided. "When I was a child, I would bring a shovel and pail and play in the sand on the beach. When I got a little older, my grandfather sometimes arranged for one of the fishermen to take me out on a boat. There's nothing quite like spending a day on the water!"

Willa shuddered at that image. "I have only been on a boat once, and that was enough for me! At least when it comes to the ocean. Boating on a lake might be tolerable, but the ocean scares me too much."

"Really?" He looked surprised, but only for a moment. "I remember you saying you did not like the ocean, but does even being on a boat bother you?"

She nodded. "In fact, being on a boat is worse than being on a beach." She studied his face for a moment, wondering whether she could trust him with the truth. She had not known him that long, after all.

But she did not see a hint of judgment or disdain in Mr. Radcliffe's face. He simply looked curious, as if he wanted to understand her. She drew a deep breath and tried to explain.

"When I'm near the ocean—whether it's a cliff like this, or the deck of a boat—I am always afraid I might fall into the water—or, worse, jump into the water—and drown."

The one time she'd ventured out in a sailboat, she had spent the whole time as far from the edge of the boat as she could. She'd sat, gripping the bench, trying not to look at the water. Her father had been very kind about her fear, but she could tell he did not understand her panic.

Nor did Mr. Radcliffe understand it now. He stared at her, his forehead wrinkled in confusion. "Why would you be afraid of jumping in? I mean, why would you even think about it? Did you *want* to jump in?"

Willa hugged herself tightly, trying to hold back the anxiety that emerged just in response to the memory. "No, of course I did not want to jump in! But I could not stop thinking about it, all the same."

She sighed, knowing no good way of explaining this. "Have you ever had a thought that kept popping into your head, even though you did not want to think about it? Even though it was something you would never actually do?"

"Yes," he replied, much to her surprise. "I do know about that. Sometimes rather terrible thoughts, too." He fell silent as he stared out towards the horizon. Then he turned to her and offered her his arm, as if he were escorting her into a ballroom. "But, you know, there are sometimes things one can do to change that."

"Of course," Willa agreed. "That's why I stay away from the ocean." Even as she spoke, she felt as if the weight in her stomach had been lifted, simply because they had turned to go back to their horses. Every step they took away from the cliff loosened her tense muscles.

He nodded. "Yes, sometimes distance is the only cure. When I was up at Cambridge, one of my friends succumbed to an illness. In my grief, I became melancholic. I had terrible thoughts that I did not want at all. In fact, my nerves became so bad, I had to leave in the middle of the term. But a few months at home helped me recover."

Willa bit her lip, struggling to hold back a series of impertinent questions. She wondered what he meant by "terrible thoughts" or when he said his nerves were "bad." But she did not have the right to ask such personal questions. If he wanted her to know, he would tell her.

"But," he continued, "I am sure it is possible to decrease one's fear of a specific object. My father had a very promising spaniel puppy who was unfortunately gun shy. Everyone told him he would have to get another shooting dog. Instead, he cut up bits of meat and took the dog out with the gamekeeper. He had the gamekeeper fire a gun, and at the same time, my father would toss the dog a bit of meat. They started off with the gun quite far away, but eventually, they worked their way up to being able to shoot near Ponto."

Willa's eyes went wide. "You mean he could work as a hunting dog?"

"Yes, except that he expected a treat every time someone fired a gun." He grinned ruefully at her. "Ponto probably wasn't the best gun dog my father ever had, but he did overcome his fear. I wonder if your fear of the ocean could be overcome that way."

She burst into laughter.

"What is so funny?" Mr. Radcliffe looked hurt.

Willa put her hands over her mouth as she struggled to stop laughing. "I'm not laughing at you!" she assured him. "I just wondered what treat you were going to toss at me in order to get me to tolerate the ocean."

The downturned corners of his mouth quirked up again. "Not raw meat, I should think. Lemon drops, perhaps?"

She giggled again. That might be his favorite sweet, but it certainly wasn't hers!

"No, wait, I have a better idea," he said gleefully. "Books by G.W. Kirkland!"

This time, they both laughed. By now, they'd reached the shady tree where the groom held their mounts. All three horses lifted their heads and stared at Willa and Mr. Radcliffe—which only made them laugh louder.

"There might be downsides to having someone chuck books at me," Willa suggested. Books were heavy, regardless of whether they were clothbound or leatherbound.

"Yes, although you might not have to worry about the book hitting you. I have very bad aim."

She snorted, and her horse snorted back, which nearly sent her off into fits of laughter again. But Willa knew that if Miss Hadfield had been here, she would have given Willa a stern look to remind her that laughing loudly and unrestrainedly was not dignified.

Even if it *was* fun.

Once they mounted their horses, Willa abandoned her amusement in order to focus on riding. Her horse, who had been quite at its ease resting in the shade, now seemed reluctant to move out into the bright sunlight.

"Not far now," Willa coaxed. The gelding flicked an ear back to listen, then picked up his speed slightly. Only then did she glance over at Mr. Radcliffe. "It is kind of you to suggest helping me, but I doubt that ridding a human of an irrational fear is as easy as training a gun-shy spaniel. People have more complicated minds than dogs."

"Perhaps." Her companion looked thoughtful. "Have you ever tried learning to swim? Maybe you would not fear jumping into the water if you knew you were in no danger of drowning."

Willa shook her head. "My mother had the same idea. One summer we stayed at an estate with a lake perfect for swimming. One of my uncles taught me to swim. I suppose it helped a little, but only a little."

She glanced towards the gray-blue ocean. The wind carried the cries of gulls far inland. By now, she associated that discordant squawking with feelings of apprehension and dread.

"I appreciate knowing that I can keep my head above water if I ever fall in," she admitted. "But even so, the ocean is frightening in a way that a lake is not." Probably Mr. Radcliffe wouldn't really understand her, but he seemed more sympathetic about her fear than most people. "Lakes aren't usually very deep, you know. They are at least fathomable. But the ocean. . . it's too big. Too deep. Unfathomable."

She drew a deep breath and tried to articulate something she'd never before put in words. "What terrified me when I was out on the boat was the fear that if I fell out, I would fall forever. It wasn't merely that I feared dying. I feared falling so deeply that my body could never be found. I have always been appalled by the idea of burial at sea. Even thinking about dropping a piece of jewelry into the water upsets me. Think of how far the bottom is, and how much time a dropped object spends falling! I don't even like thinking about how vast the ocean is."

Too embarrassed to meet Mr. Radcliffe's gaze, she stared intently at the space between her horse's ears. What she did not say was that when she'd been younger, she had feared that the ocean might genuinely be limitless, that a thing tossed overboard would literally fall forever. The very idea petrified her.

"I hadn't thought of that before," Mr. Radcliffe admitted. "I mean, I have wondered how deep the deepest parts of the ocean are. And wondered how far down sea life may be found, for that matter. But I never considered the depths of the ocean as a source of ontological dread."

Willa, who had only a vague idea of what "ontological dread" might mean, glanced doubtfully over at Mr. Radcliffe. He simultaneously turned his head to look at her, and their eyes met. For a single charged moment, it felt as if some unspoken sign passed between them.

Willa's heartbeat sped from a walk to a gallop. Unsettled, she glanced away, pretending to be preoccupied by the smooth gravel track before them.

"It is an interesting question," Mr. Radcliffe added. "And an interesting problem. I wonder how one could solve it?"

"Solve it?" In her surprise, Willa raised her voice so much that her placid horse snorted and tossed his head uneasily. Now she really did have to devote all her attention to calming her mount. Once the horse settled, she resumed the conversation. "It is kind of you to wish to help me, Mr. Radcliffe, but I do not think it is a problem that can be solved. Nor did I intend to appeal to you for assistance."

"Of course, if you wish me to leave the matter alone, I will do so," he assured her. "But I like interesting challenges, and this one is more intriguing than sea glass. I would like to think more on the subject. Would you mind if I did so?"

Willa's mouth hung ajar for an awkward moment. She closed it and gave her startled wits a shake to get them in order. "Your mind is your own realm, sir. You are welcome to think about the problem as much or as little as you please. But even if you find a possible solution, I cannot commit to pursuing it. Sometimes it is better to leave a knotty problem alone, lest it become further tangled." She could not imagine what could make her fear even worse, but anything was possible.

"Naturally, you do not have to act on any solution I propose," he agreed. "I may not even come up with a good solution. I am not, after all, an expert on the workings of the human mind. But I promise to inform you if I do think of anything that might help you move past your phobia."

"Very well," Willa said. "I appreciate your thoughtfulness." It would, after all, be nice to enjoy the seaside the way other people did. A fear of the ocean was most inconvenient for someone who lived in an island nation!

She felt certain, though, that this puzzle would remain un-solved. Other people had tried to help Willa overcome her unreasonable fear. How likely was it that Mr. Radcliffe would succeed where her own family had failed?

Chapter Thirteen

T HE NEXT DAY, Aunt Faith sent Ben into town on an errand. While he talked to the shopkeeper about the hat trimmings his aunt wanted, he heard a familiar voice behind him. He stole a covert glance over his shoulder to confirm that Mrs. Trimmer had just entered the store.

Once he completed his millinery purchases, Ben waylaid Mrs. Trimmer. He skipped over the customary exchange of pleasantries and asked, "I say, do you happen to know what Lady Wilhelmina's favorite sweet is? Something smaller than a cake, I mean."

Mrs. Trimmer looked taken aback, but she recovered quickly. "I believe Lady Wilhelmina is very fond of lavender." Her face relaxed into a smile.

"Lavender? Isn't that used for cosmetics or something?" He knew little about perfume, but he vaguely remembered that women sometimes used lavender water instead of rose water as a scent.

"Oh, yes. But you can cook with lavender, too. Willa is very fond of lavender biscuits."

"I see!" Where on earth could Ben find lavender biscuits, though? He had never seen them at Plummer's Bakery.

Fortunately, Mrs. Trimmer anticipated his dilemma. "I can send your aunt my recipe, if you like. Or have my cook give it to your Mrs. Kirby. Would you like that?"

"Yes, please." He beamed at her. "That would be perfect!"

He felt confident that his grandfather's cook could handle something as simple as making lavender biscuits. At least, he assumed it was simple. Didn't every cook know how to bake biscuits and cakes?

Soon, he'd have all the components needed for his experiment.

Only after Ben left the shop did it occur to him that Mrs. Trimmer probably knew nothing about his plan to help Lady Wilhelmina overcome her phobia. She would, therefore, not understand why he needed to know Lady Wilhelmina's favorite biscuits. What must she think? Did she expect him to show up at the door with a tin of biscuits and a confession of his undying love?

Oh, dear. He'd probably put his foot in it, but he saw no way of mending the error now. He'd have to hope that Lady Wilhelmina explained the real situation to her cousin.

A FEW DAYS later, Ben's aunt made one of her rare visits to his workroom. She held a folded piece of paper and wore a thoughtful frown. "Ben, may I speak with you?"

Her voice startled him out of a brown study. "Yes? Did you need something?"

She almost never came out here; that had been an implicit part of the agreement when he took over this space. He would keep his seashells, fossils, and dead sea horses out of the house, and his aunt would leave him in peace.

"Ben, did you want me to make these biscuits for my next afternoon at home? Do the Selwyn ladies intend to drop by?"

"What?" He stared at her, more than half his mind still occupied with the letter he'd been reading. "What biscuits?"

His aunt looked amused. "Now, that's more like you. I mean the lavender biscuits. Mrs. Trimmer said you asked her for the recipe."

"Oh, that!" Ben returned his aunt's smile. "No, I was going to use that for training."

"Training?" Aunt Faith wrinkled her brow.

"Not literally *training*," Ben clarified. "But you know how people train dogs using praise and treats?"

"Yes?" For some reason, she looked worried. "What does that have to do with Lady Wilhelmina's favorite biscuits?"

Ben tried to explain about his friend's fear of the ocean and his father's method for training gun dogs, but the longer he talked, the more concerned Aunt Faith grew. By the time he reached the end of his explanation, her smile had fled entirely, and the worried wrinkle in her brow had deepened.

"And so," he concluded, "I thought if she associated the ocean with something she liked, such as her favorite sweet, she might grow to tolerate it, the way Ponto eventually learned to tolerate the sound of gunfire." He smiled hopefully.

Aunt Faith sank down into an empty chair, as if her legs could no longer support her, and proceeded to scold him. "Benjamin Radcliffe, of all the preposterous ideas I have heard from you over the years, this may be the worst. You cannot train a girl the way you would train a dog! Why, the very idea is profoundly disrespectful."

Ben crossed his arms over his chest and returned her frown with one of his own. "I do not see how it is disrespectful to help Lady Wilhelmina. Her fear of the ocean prevents her from enjoying the best that Newell-on-Sea has to offer. If she learned to tolerate it, she might enjoy her stay here much more than she does now. She has already told me she does not mind me trying to find a solution." It was not as if he were forcing unwanted help on her!

It was clear that Lady Wilhelmina's dislike of the ocean prevented her from fully benefiting from a seaside resort. She had, after all, been so bored and unhappy that she took the unusual step of throwing a message for help over the edge of a cliff. Why, that was like *asking* for Ben's help!

His aunt rested her head in hands before responding. "Ben, I assure you that there are better ways to ensure that Lady Wilhelmina enjoys her seaside holiday. Why don't you invite her to go riding with you again? Or escort her to one of the assemblies in Caseton? Or, you know, you might call upon her at her cousin's house, the way a normal person would."

Ben dropped his gaze. A lump formed in his throat, making it difficult for him to mutter, "I am not a normal person, aunt. You must know that by now."

"Oh, dear." She patted him gently on the shoulder. "I did not mean to offend you, Benjamin. I know you are not interested in the usual things that keep young people entertained. But sometimes one has to make concessions. There are times when it is necessary to do as other people do, if only to get what one wants."

Ben jerked back from her, shoving his chair away from the table. "Do you think I haven't heard that before?" He had heard it all his life, especially from his father. Sir Lewis frequently advised Ben to behave more like other gentlemen his age, whether that meant pretending to be interested in field sports or dressing more fashionably.

"I do not believe this is a case where I should pretend to be somebody else," he insisted. "I want Lady Wilhelmina to like me as I am, or not at all! And I am most certainly not going to kick my heels up at one of those dreadful assemblies in Caseton, where the instruments aren't even in tune."

His aunt threw her hands in the air. "One time! The pianoforte was out of tune only ONE TIME! It is not fair to hold that against Mr. Courteney forever."

Ben tightened his lips. He thought it was *entirely* fair to blame the Master of Ceremonies for not having the instrument tuned before an assembly. It was Mr. Courteney's job to make certain that everything went smoothly at those dances.

Aunt Faith visibly struggled to calm herself. "Besides," she said more gently, "wouldn't you like a chance to dance with your new acquaintance?"

"No," Ben said bluntly. "I do not want to dance with any-one." To be sure, he would not have minded having an excuse to hold Lady Wilhelmina's hand. But even that possibility could not tempt him to return to an overheated assembly room where he could hardly hear himself think.

His aunt released a long-suffering sigh. "Very well. If you really wish to spend a day on the beach, we could arrange for a walk and a picnic lunch. But you ought to invite some other young people to make a nice party, and—"

Ben's jaw dropped. "I don't want to have a *party*." He only wanted to spend time with Lady Wilhelmina. His shoulders slumped when he remembered how impossible that was. "I suppose I could invite her sister and their governess along to gather shells with me." That would satisfy the proprieties, but it would be difficult to put his plan in action with other people hanging about.

"I suppose that will do. But I would have thought you might like to introduce your friends to some of the local society." His aunt shook her head.

Ben could not see why Aunt Faith sounded so disappointed. She ought to know by now that Ben had no intention of entering into the regular rounds of dinner parties, card parties, and private balls hosted by the local gentry. Unless. . . he stared thoughtfully down at the table.

"You don't suppose the Selwyn ladies particularly *want* to be introduced to other local families, do you?" he asked cautiously. "They are only here for their health, after all. It is not as if they intend to permanently take up residence in Newell."

She scowled at him. "Benjamin Radcliffe, do you or do not hope to persuade Lady Wilhelmina to stay here after her mother's holiday ends?"

Ben stared at his aunt. "What? Why would I do that? She doesn't even like the seaside." He hoped to make the ocean more tolerable for her, but there was no guarantee that his plan would work.

Aunt Faith threw her hands in the air. "Evidently, I misunderstood the situation. Please, forget that I said anything. I shall send a note around inviting Mrs. Trimmer and her houseguests to a picnic on the beach, shall I?"

"Not on the beach," he corrected. "Above it. Perhaps on top of the point. That would be better than being right on the water." Lady Wilhelmina's phobia apparently did not prevent her from exploring the cliffs above the beach.

"Very well. Above the beach. I suppose we will have to hope for good weather." She turned towards the door.

"Don't forget the lavender biscuits!" Ben called after her. "The whole thing will be pointless without them."

His aunt glanced back over her shoulder and shook her head, smiling ruefully, but she said only, "Lavender biscuits it is!"

What a strange conversation! Ben returned to his chair and picked up the letter he'd been reading. But try as he might, he could not focus on it. He kept thinking about what his aunt had said. Why would she think he wanted to persuade any of the Selwyn family to stay at Newell?

Oh. When he worked it out, he felt foolish. Aunt Faith assumed that he wanted to marry Lady Wilhelmina and to live with her at Marlowe Tower. That was why she wanted him to introduce Lady Wilhelmina to local families.

Which was nonsense. True, Ben would have to marry someone eventually, since he had no younger brothers to carry on the family name. But whether he married Lady Wilhelmina Selwyn or someone else, he would presumably bring his bride home to Coville Hall. There was no dower house on the Radcliffe family estate, but his father had promised the currently unoccupied steward's cottage to Ben.

It was, to say the least, extremely unlikely that Ben would live at Marlowe Tower after his marriage. True, he was half Marlowe, but he wasn't the only Marlowe grandchild, nor even the oldest of them. Almeria and Marlowe Millington were both older than Ben. Probably one of them would inherit. Unlike the Radcliffe properties, the Marlowe estate was not included. Ben's grandfather was free to bequeath it to whomever he pleased.

Would Grandfather really leave his estate to Marlowe Millington, though? Marlowe had never shown the least interest in the family holdings. He might be interested in spending the family fortune, but Ben had difficulty imagining him as either a conscientious landlord or a wise investor.

However, that was Grandfather's concern, not Ben's. Someday managing the Radcliffe land gave Ben enough to worry about. But for the rest of the day, the question kept nagging him: Who was Grandfather Marlowe's heir, anyway?

Chapter Fourteen

FORTUNE SMILED ON the Selwyn family. After several days of overcast skies, the sun broke through on the first Saturday in June, scattering beams of golden light across the Dorset coast.

Even better, Willa's mother finally felt well enough to accept invitations. Lady Inglewhite's cough no longer bothered her, except at night, and some of the bloom returned to her face. She chose the picnic at Marlowe Tower for her first outing since her illness.

"It really could not be better weather for a picnic," Cousin Sarah announced. She settled down in a corner of the rear-facing carriage seat.

Cousin Sarah carried an enormous wicker basket loaded with her contributions to the day's feast, and she insisted on carrying it for herself, though both Willa and Miss Hadfield had offered to help.

Willa, intent on being useful, sat next to Cousin Sarah. Phoebe plopped down next to her, grinning broadly.

"Do you think we'll get to walk on the beach today?" Phoebe had already asked that question at least twice this morning, so Miss Hadfield could perhaps be forgiven for answering with only a shrug of her shoulders and a slight smile.

"I doubt it," Willa warned. "Mr. Radcliffe knows I prefer to avoid the ocean."

"Assuming he remembers," Mama gently reminded Willa. "I hope you will be gracious about his invitation even if he does plan for us to explore the cove. The ocean *is* what draws people to Newell, after all."

"Yes, I know." Willa stared down at the tips of her half-boots. He would remember; she felt certain of that. How could he forget after their conversation about the ocean? By now, she was a little embarrassed to think about how much she'd said about her phobia.

But Mr. Radcliffe might have allowed other considerations to overrule any concern he felt for Willa. She was not, after all, the only guest at this picnic. Besides, the invitation had come from Miss Marlowe rather than Mr. Radcliffe. For all Willa knew, her friend might have little say in the planning. Miss Marlowe probably knew nothing about Willa's fear of the ocean.

When they reached the Tower, though, they discovered that the outdoor meal had been set up on Castle Rock Point rather than on the beach below. Everyone smiled, uttered polite greetings, and looked uncertain about what to say next. At least, Willa felt awkward. She suspected Mr. Radcliffe did, too.

Willa's mother gratefully sank down onto the wrought-iron bench. Stationing the picnickers here had been good thinking on someone's part. It meant not everyone had to sit on the picnic blanket.

Cousin Sarah joined Lady Inglewhite on the bench. "Old bones are not meant to sit on the damp ground," she explained. "I leave that to you young people."

Mr. Radcliffe's aunt chuckled. "I did not expect to be lumped in with the young people today! I rather doubt I can keep up with them." She smiled pleasantly at both Selwyn sisters, but her gaze lingered on Willa.

"Yes, keeping up with youngsters can be quite a challenge," Miss Hadfield agreed. "Especially when the young people have been fueled by sweets." She looked pointedly at the basket Willa was unpacking and arched a single eyebrow.

"It's not all sweets," Mr. Radcliffe said. "There are a couple of cheeses and some plain biscuits here, too. See?" He squatted down beside his own hamper of food and began lifting items out, beginning with a wedge of Dorset Blue Vinny, followed by cheddar.

Mr. Radcliffe's dog looked up at his master beseechingly and whined. His master glanced down and shook his finger. "Be good, Cato."

Cato gazed longingly at the plate of cheese, but he sat still rather than lunging towards the food the way some dogs would have done.

Still, Willa predicted trouble in the near future. In her experience, dogs and picnics did not mix well. She opened her mouth, intending to suggest that Cato should be tied well away from the food to prevent theft, but at the last moment she reconsidered. It was not her place to tell Mr. Radcliffe how to handle his dog. Maybe Cato really *would* be good.

Doing her best to ignore the whining mongrel, Willa settled down on one of the padded cushions that had been brought out for the picnic. She started to unpack Cousin Sarah's basket, but something else caught her attention.

"Oh, and you brought fruit, too. I did not know there were any strawberries ripe yet!" Willa nabbed one of the smaller berries, which looked and smelled as if it had been picked at the perfect stage. She took a cautious nibble and discovered that, wonder of wonders, it tasted every bit as sweet as it looked. The rest of the berry vanished in one bite.

"Those are from my grandfather's succession houses," Mr. Radcliffe explained. "I daresay the field-grown strawberries are not yet ripe."

Finally, Mr. Radcliffe pulled a heavy-looking fruitcake out of the hamper. Willa could smell the rum from a foot away. "Goodness, that's powerful," she murmured.

Mr. Radcliffe scrunched up his face in disgust. "My cousin Almeria made this, using her mother's recipe. Grandfather used to love that fruitcake, but he finds it doesn't agree with him anymore. He thought we might like to share it, since he cannot eat it." He set the dessert down on a plate well away from both of them.

"That's a good idea." Willa infused as much enthusiasm into her voice as she could, though the cake did not look particularly appealing. She did not care for currants or citron, and it looked like this cake contained both.

They had just finished unpacking Cousin Sarah's basket when a strong gust of wind blew across the point. The breeze yanked Phoebe's bonnet off. Phoebe yelped, sprang to her feet, and ran after it.

Mama released a soft, ladylike peal of laughter as Phoebe and Willa gave chase to the errant headgear. Unfortunately, Cato reached the bonnet before they did. He grabbed it, shook it vigorously, and threw a play bow at Willa and Phoebe.

"Nice doggie!" Phoebe said. "Give me my hat back!"

Cato wagged his tail. For a moment, it looked as if he would let Phoebe take the bonnet. But just before she could reach for it, he galloped away. He glanced back over his shoulder to make sure they followed him. Clearly, he had in mind a merry game.

Willa and Phoebe wasted several minutes chasing Cato, to no avail. His plumed tail waved triumphantly. He seemed to be having the time of his life.

"Cato!" Mr. Radcliffe called. "I've got a treat for you!" He held up a morsel of something small, impossible to identify at this distance.

The dog came to an abrupt halt. He perked his ears up and stared intently at Mr. Radcliffe. Then he dropped Phoebe's bonnet on the ground and trotted over to get his reward.

Phoebe quickly snatched up her bonnet, only to make a face and exclaim, "Eww! It's all slobbery!"

Mama laughed, though not unkindly. "That is why you must remember to tie the ribbons tightly each time you put it on," she reminded Phoebe. "The wind would not have taken your bonnet if you had properly secured it."

Phoebe released a theatrical sigh and reluctantly placed the bonnet (looking much worse for the wear) on her head. Meanwhile, the dog who had caused so much trouble obediently sat down at Mr. Radcliffe's command. He looked like butter wouldn't melt in his mouth—whatever that meant.

"I am very sorry about that." Mr. Radcliffe's cheeks had flushed a faint pink. "I am afraid Cato is not very well trained." His eyes met Willa's and for some reason, his blush deepened. "Perhaps we had better enjoy the food before Cato gets it."

That was a suggestion with which everyone could agree. Willa started with cheese and plain biscuits, then moved on to strawberries and cream. She was about to conclude her meal with a sweet roll when she saw Miss Marlowe nudge her nephew and murmur something in his ear.

Mr. Radcliffe opened up a small tin. "Lady Wilhelmina, my aunt made those lavender biscuits you like." He offered the tin to Willa, smiling bashfully.

"Thank you. That was very thoughtful of you." Willa reached for the tin, but as Mr. Radcliffe passed it over, her ungloved fingers brushed against his. Willa flinched at the unexpected contact, and she fumbled the tin, nearly dumping its contents onto the grass.

All eyes seemed to be watching her clumsiness. "I am not usually so maladroit!" she said, trying to laugh it off.

"Perhaps the sun got in your eyes," Miss Marlowe suggested.

It was kindly meant, but it seemed an unlikely explanation. Willa merely nodded and took a bite of one of the biscuits. Everyone watched her eat, waiting for her reaction. A lull in the conversation meant her chewing sounded unnaturally loud, at least to her ears. Her mouth had gone dry, and she struggled to swallow the bite, until Miss Hadfield handed her a cup of tea.

Goodness, was her opinion really that important? The silence suggested it was. Fortunately, Willa could deliver a favorable verdict. "It is perfect," she announced. "It tastes just like the biscuits Cousin Sarah makes."

She took another sip of tea and relaxed as conversation finally resumed. What was *that* all about? One would think she were a taste-tester evaluating a candidate for the role of head cook in King George's household.

After everyone had finished eating and the food had been packed away, most of the party took the staircase down to the beach. Willa stayed on the cliff, pretending to enjoy the "light breeze" that threatened to do with her bonnet what it had done with Phoebe's.

She sat in awkward solitude, realizing she ought to have brought a book. One should *always* bring a book. It was most unfortunate that so few books were small enough to be tucked into a pocket or reticule. A publisher who specialized in pocket-sized editions of popular novels could make a fortune.

To her surprise, Mr. Radcliffe returned before the rest of the group. "I did not think it right for all of us to abandon you," he explained.

"That was very thoughtful of you." She smiled up at him. . . and then kept smiling foolishly as he stood beside the bench, silently looking down at her. "Won't you have a seat?" she prompted at last.

"Oh! Yes!" He sat beside her, but kept his eyes fixed on the closed hampers of leftovers. "I wanted to explain my plan for today, even though you'll probably be offended."

Willa stared at him. "Why would I be offended?"

He watched her warily out of the corner of his eyes. "Because I originally intended to use those lavender biscuits to help you overcome your fear of the ocean," he explained.

She wrinkled her forehead. "How would biscuits help me overcome—oh! You mean like your father's gun dog?" That half-forgotten conversation came back to her now.

He finally looked her in the eye. "Precisely. I thought maybe if you ate something you enjoyed in close proximity to the ocean, you would build pleasant associations with it. You know, like what Wordsworth says about the overbalance of pleasure in the Preface to *Lyrical Ballads*."

Willa blinked and tried to remember any of Wordsworth's ideas. She gave up and shook her head. "I am afraid I do not remember that part of the Preface."

"He said people could listen to a tragic story that might be painful, but the pain would be balanced out by the beauty of the poetry," Mr. Radcliffe explained.

"But what does that have to do with dog training?" Willa felt thoroughly lost.

Mr. Radcliffe grinned at her. "Nothing to do with dogs," he admitted. "But Wordsworth thought people developed such strong positive associations with regular meter that they experienced pleasure just from reading metered poetry. Therefore, if they heard a painful story told in formal verse, the pleasing qualities of the meter would balance out the painful feelings the subject aroused."

"Oh. You have a better memory than I do." She hadn't remembered that part of the essay at all, though Miss Hadfield had once made Willa spend an entire afternoon dissecting Wordsworth's theory of prosody.

He shrugged. "I either remember nothing about what I read, or everything about it, depending on how interesting it is. As it happens, Wordsworth interested me. I thought his theory explained why I preferred the work of modern poets to those of the previous generation. But I digress."

He smiled ruefully. "In any case, I thought perhaps lavender biscuits could create an 'overbalance of pleasure' that would allow you to more easily tolerate proximity to the ocean."

"I see." Willa bit her lip. "In that case, the gesture was even more thoughtful than I realized. It was very good of you to try to help me."

"You aren't offended?" he asked anxiously. "Aunt Faith thought it was disrespectful of me to train you as if you were a dog. That's why I didn't say anything earlier, but—"

Willa burst into a fit of giggles. Once she got her laughter under control, she said, "No, I am not offended. But I think it would take more than a biscuit to make me like the ocean. You must offer a more enticing prize."

"Such as?" He looked her earnestly in the face. "If a biscuit isn't incentive enough, what *would* entice you?"

He was serious about this, wasn't he? Willa bit her lip, holding back another urge to giggle. Until he leaned forward a little, close enough for her to see the darker rings of green around his jade-colored eyes.

Her heart fluttered, and the urge to laugh vanished. She might have been imagining things, but Mr. Radcliffe looked to be on the verge of kissing her. She closed her eyes and tipped her chin up, just in case it wasn't her imagination.

But the expected kiss never came.

Chapter Fifteen

WHY DID LADY Wilhelmina close her eyes? Maybe Ben was sitting too close to her. But if that were the case, wouldn't she simply move farther away? If anything, he thought she might have leaned in a bit closer.

Ben's heart thumped unevenly. If he leaned forward and slanted his mouth down, he could easily kiss her . . . but of course, she would probably slap him if he did that.

Or would she? *What if she wanted him to kiss her?* It couldn't hurt to ask. Unless it did hurt, of course.

Before he could shape his amorphous thoughts into a coherent sentence, disaster struck.

"Mr. Radcliffe!" a voice called. "We need your assistance!"

Just like that, all the romance of the moment melted away. Ben closed his eyes as disappointment weighed him down. Then he pushed his feelings aside and opened his eyes again. The urgency in the governess's voice meant he had more important things to worry about than kissing.

"Yes, Miss Hadfield?" He rose to his feet and hurried to meet her. "What is wrong? Did someone get hurt?" Fear turned his trot into a jog. What if Lady Phoebe had played too close to the ocean and—

"Your aunt is very sick," Miss Hadfield explained. "A sudden stomach upset. She may need your help to get back to the house."

Stomach trouble again? A shiver ran down Ben's spine. An ominous possibility hovered just past the reach of conscious thought. But the idea, whatever it might be, vanished as soon as he tried to capture it.

No matter. If the idea was important, it would return.

For now, Aunt Faith needed him. He found her sitting halfway up the stone staircase that connected the sandy cove to the cliffs above. Doubled over in pain, she had already vomited once and looked as if she were about to be sick again.

"I can help you move her," Miss Hadfield suggested. "It might be best if Lady Inglewhite and the others go back to the village, so they won't be in our way."

She stared at him, but it still took entirely too long for him to realize that she was waiting for him to make a decision. With his aunt unwell, all the responsibility of hosting the gathering fell on his inexperienced shoulders.

He lifted his chin, hoping he looked more confident than he felt. "Yes, that might be best. There is no need to keep everyone standing around while I take my aunt home. If you will assist me in getting my aunt back to the house, we can send you home in our carriage later, Miss Hadfield." He did not like drafting one of the guests into sick duties, but it would have been difficult to get his aunt home without help.

He made a hasty apology to the other concerned guests, then helped his aunt walk back to the Tower. Even with Miss Hadfield's help, the journey was a difficult one.

There were few things that drew Grandfather Marlowe out of his study in the middle of the afternoon, but today he abandoned his writing to hover over his daughter's bedside.

"Have you sent for the doctor?" Grandfather kept asking, though the answer remained the same.

"Yes, Grandfather," Ben assured him. "I sent for Dr. Milner."

He knew, though, that it might take hours to locate the physician. The closest alternative was the local apothecary, but the treatments Mr. Chapman had offered Grandfather Marlowe's dyspepsia had never been very effective. Ben saw no point in summoning him now.

As the hours ticked by, Aunt Faith's condition worsened. Just as in the case of Ben's illness a few weeks ago, her vomiting was followed by a violent flux. The housekeeper, Mrs. Smith, suggested that they try administering the same colic medicine Ben had taken when he was last ill.

This seemed to help. By the time Dr. Milner finally arrived, Aunt Faith had gotten over the worst of the diarrhea. Ben, hoping for a good prognosis, watched anxiously as Dr. Milner put his stethoscope to the patient's chest and listened.

When the doctor lifted his head, he still looked grave, and some of Ben's optimism faded.

"Her heartbeat is quite erratic," Dr. Milner warned. "That may be a result of the lowering effects of the vomiting and diarrhea. We can try to treat those symptoms—the colic medicine was a good idea. Keep administering that. In addition, make sure she drinks plenty of water. If her stomach will allow it, some beef tea may also be given. I dare not prognosticate as to how this case may develop."

Grandfather Marlowe shook his head. "I thought at first that Faith had finally inherited my tendency towards dyspepsia. But she is far sicker than I ever was. I cannot remember the last time anyone in the household was this unwell!"

Ben frowned. "I don't know. This seems much like the gastritis I had back in April. It took me a few days to recover, but I am perfectly well now!" Hopefully, Aunt Faith would recover just as quickly.

But when he glanced at the doctor, hoping to see some sign that he shared Ben's optimism, Dr. Milner's expression remained grim.

"You are also more than twenty years younger than Miss Marlowe," the physician reminded Ben, "and you generally enjoy good health. That can make an enormous difference in a case like this, you know."

"I see." He turned back towards his aunt. "We must make sure you rest, Aunt Faith."

A brief smile flashed across her exhausted face. "I can hardly do anything else at the moment."

So strange to see her laid low this way! She was older than Ben's mother, but she remained quite active, and illnesses rarely kept her down for long.

Dr. Milner cleared his throat. "Now, if you gentlemen have no other questions, I do have a patient in Newell to visit—"

Ben interrupted him. "I do have one question." He hesitated, not certain that this was the right time to ask.

"Yes?" Dr. Milner said encouragingly.

"Why do we keep having attacks of gastritis?" Ben asked. "Surely it isn't common for two people in the same household to have attacks a month apart, is it?"

"We're coming on summer now," Grandfather Marlowe pointed out. "Quite common for people to have stomach upsets in the summer, isn't it?" He glanced expectantly towards Dr. Milner, waiting for the physician's confirmation.

Ben, on the other hand, uneasily shifted his weight from one foot to another. He did not want to contradict his grandfather, but that explanation didn't make sense to him. In Ben's experience, most seasonal illnesses came in clusters. A whole household might fall sick in a matter of days. But Aunt Faith's gastric attack had occurred weeks after Ben's sickness.

Dr. Milner frowned. "As I am sure you know, many diseases are communicable. If your gastritis was caused by a miasma, the same thing might have struck your aunt. Or there might be some problem in the kitchen. Many a stomach upset has been caused by food gone off or meals improperly prepared."

"Yes," Grandfather Marlowe agreed. "That probably accounts for it. I have heard of whole households falling ill because of a single rancid dish. I shall have a talk with the cook." He smiled down at his daughter and patted her hand. "We shall have you up and well in no time, Faith."

"I hope it is as simple as that," Ben said, but he remained skeptical. There had been no change in the kitchen staff this spring. It did not make sense for a cook and a kitchen maid who had prepared perfectly wholesome meals in the past to suddenly begin producing tainted food.

"For now, we must hope for the best." Dr. Milner patted Ben on the shoulder. That gesture, more than anything else, indicated how concerned he was.

THE NEXT DAY, Aunt Faith showed little improvement. Her stomach could handle only beef tea and dry toast, and she continued to complain that her heart "fluttered" and skipped beats. None of this sounded at all promising, but Ben tried to keep his pessimism to himself.

He sat with his aunt for an hour in the morning, reading from one of her favorite collections of poetry, *Lavender and Lilacs*. Ben did not understand half of the flowery metaphors, but there was something satisfying about the regular rhyme and meter. More evidence that Wordsworth's theories were correct, perhaps?

"It's a pity that I ruined your picnic," his aunt said. "I know you were looking forward to it. Please tell your guests how sorry I am."

"You didn't ruin it!" Ben protested. "You merely caused it to end a little sooner than expected, and I am sure neither Mrs. Trimmer nor her cousins hold you to blame. But if you like, I will convey your apologies to them."

He might believe the apology to be unnecessary, but it gave him an opportunity to write to Lady Wilhelmina, or rather, to her family. There was, he supposed, no way that he could send a note specifically to his friend.

Not unless he wrote it in between the lines.

Normally, Ben preferred direct communication. He would

rather say what he meant than hint or beat around the bush. He was not at all sure that Lady Wilhelmina would understand his cryptic hints, but he could think of no better way to communicate.

After he explained about his aunt's illness and passed along her regrets, he added a paragraph specifically for her.

It is a pity that Lady Wilhelmina left before we could test my theory about dog training. I am sure that if a springer spaniel can be taught not to be anxious around guns, a water spaniel can learn not to fear water. The question is, what reward might provide sufficient encouragement? I will continue to investigate. It might help if I explored other locations, rather than confining myself to the cove. This Thursday, I plan to take Cato to Newell beach rather than to the cove for his morning walk. Perhaps the new location might lead to a new solution. Who knows what we might find there?

He read over the paragraph, knowing it might not be clear enough. Even if Lady Wilhelmina recognized his attempt to arrange a meeting, she might not approve of such a clandestine rendezvous. She had more to lose than Ben did, a lady's reputation being so fragile.

But he could think of no better plan, so he signed the letter, sealed it, and sent it into town with one of the footmen. Then he cracked open the door of his aunt's room and peered inside. She slept, though the foul smell lingering in the room indicated that some of her digestive symptoms must have recurred. Maybe she needed another dose of medicine.

Ben did not enter the room—he did not want to wake his aunt. Instead, he hovered in the doorway and watched her sleep. He wished he could share his grandfather's optimism, but all he could think of was the somber expression on Dr. Milner's face.

Aunt Faith's initial symptoms had seemed similar to Ben's previous illness, but surely, he had never looked so stricken, so weak. His heart had never skipped beats or fallen out of rhythm.

He'd only had an upset stomach, the sort of thing that could happen to anyone.

What, he wondered, could have made his aunt so sick, so suddenly?

Chapter Sixteen

"A RE YOU SURE you want to go for a walk today?" Phoebe peered out the window, studying the overcast sky. "It looks like it might rain, and that wind will make for a rough sea."

Willa smiled. Since when did Phoebe uses phrases like "rough sea"? Maybe she'd started picking up nautical language from the locals. By now, Phoebe had become fast friends with a girl her own age who lived a few houses down from Cousin Sarah.

"We probably will not stay out very long," Willa assured her sister. "If the weather grows too bad, we can return home. And I will be prepared in case of rain." She lifted up the umbrella she'd taken from the hat stand near the front door.

"Even if it doesn't rain, the wind is still cold," Phoebe complained. "I would much rather wait until the sun comes out. Maybe the afternoon will be better?"

Willa hesitated and scanned the entryway, making sure no one else could hear them. "If you feel so strongly about it," she said quietly, "you may stay home. It is a pity Miss Hadfield is not available, but I do not need an escort. In the country, you know, it is perfectly acceptable for a young lady to walk alone."

She held her breath as she waited for her sister to decide. She did not want to say too much to convince Phoebe to stay home. This must be Phoebe's decision. It might look suspicious if Willa actively tried to leave her sister behind, especially since Miss

Hadfield could not take Phoebe's place.

"If you really don't mind, I believe I will stay home," Phoebe decided. "I wanted to do some reading today, anyway." She wrinkled her nose. "It's a boring old history book, but I promised Haddy I would try to finish it."

A smile bloomed across Willa's face. Phoebe had just given her the perfect excuse for walking by herself. Miss Hadfield would hardly complain when she learned that her pupil had stayed behind to study history. On the contrary, she'd be delighted. Unlike Willa, Phoebe was no great reader.

Anticipation warred with anxiety as Willa left the house and turned down High Street, walking briskly toward Newell Bay. She drew a deep breath and caught the faint scent of rain, overladen with the stronger odor of the sea. Phoebe was probably right to worry about the weather.

She worried that Mr. Radcliffe might have taken one look at the overcast sky and decided not to wander so far from home. Or he might have already come and gone. She could not expect him to linger on the beach all morning in the hope of encountering her. This might well be a wasted walk.

Or not.

As soon as Willa turned onto the stone walkway that skirted the beach, she saw him. Or rather, *them.* Mr. Radcliffe's brown-and-white dog trotted by his side, ears lifted and tail wagging. When Cato caught sight of Willa, he dropped his jaw to display a canine grin.

Willa stepped more quickly as she hurried to join them. Fortunately, Mr. Radcliffe met her on the stone walkway, so she did not have to walk through the sand. The gritty feel of sand in her shoes might be only a minor annoyance, but she would still rather avoid it.

Avoiding the presence of the ocean was harder. The wind drove the sea against the curving harbor wall, making the rumble and crash of the waves louder than ever. She kept her eyes fixed on Mr. Radcliffe and his dog, refusing to look out over the water.

Her neck already ached from the strain.

"Lady Wilhelmina! Fancy meeting you here!" Mr. Radcliffe's eyes were wide with surprise—too wide, in fact.

She bit back a snicker. That exaggerated look of surprise would not have convinced anyone. But the smile with which he greeted her seemed both warm and genuine. So warm, in fact, that it made Willa's heart briefly flutter.

Or maybe that was indigestion. Who could say? Either way, she smiled broadly back. She had not misread his letter. He really did want her to meet him here.

But now that they were face-to-face, without a chaperone at hand, she was not sure what he expected of her.

When in doubt, Willa decided, be direct.

"Why did you want to meet me here, Mr. Radcliffe?" Too late, she realized the words might sound accusatory, so she softened them. "Was there something particular you wished to discuss?"

"Ah, yes." He flicked his gaze in the direction of the turbulent ocean before turning back to Willa. "Does it upset you to be so close to the water?"

"I try to avoid looking at it," Willa admitted. Or thinking about it, for that matter. "Though it is not possible to ignore the sound or smell of it. But being here is not as bad as being out on a boat." Nothing in the world was as bad as that.

"Do you think you could tolerate spending a quarter of an hour here? Not just today, but regularly?"

Willa frowned. "Tolerate, yes. Enjoy it, no. Especially not today." She owed only part of her shiver to the driving wind. "You must admit that the sea is not at all tame today."

"No, I suppose it is not." He made a face. "It would hardly be pleasant to sit on the beach and read in this weather. Most unfortunate."

"Read?" She stared at him blankly.

"Oh, right, I never had a chance to explain that part! You said the other day that sweet biscuits were not reward enough to lure you near the ocean."

"Yes, I did say that." Willa blushed. As it happened, he'd gotten her to the beach without mentioning any reward. She had come because she wanted to see *him*.

"Well, I thought of a better prize." He opened up the satchel at his side and pulled out a leather-bound volume, which he handed to Willa.

She gasped. "*Terror at Carringford Park*! Where did you get this? I thought the bookstore sold all their copies."

"They did," he agreed. "So I asked Miss Thatcher to order a copy of it for you. This is just the first volume, of course, but I got the whole novel. I thought we could read it together by the ocean, and maybe. . ." He let his voice trail off. Then he shrugged, looking sheepish. "Maybe you would come to associate the beach with one of your favorite authors?" He stole a quick glance at her, then shifted his eyes away, as if he were too bashful to look her directly in the face.

"You really are the sweetest man!" she blurted out.

He stared at her, wide-eyed, for a painful moment that felt like an eternity. She had rendered him speechless!

Unfortunately, he wasn't the only one who found himself tongue-tied. Willa frantically searched for some way to backtrack from the unexpected compliment, but she was afraid that if she opened her mouth, she would start babbling. Better to say nothing at all than to blather on.

"The feeling's mutual, you know. That is to say, I like you, too." He blinked owlishly, looking about as perplexed as Willa felt. "What I mean is—"

Before he could muddle his answer any further, his dog barked at him. Willa immediately lowered her eyes, relieved to have a good distraction. She stroked Cato's soft head and hoped Mr. Radcliffe wasn't going to declare himself yet. She was not yet certain how she would answer him.

"Cato's probably annoyed that I stopped walking," Mr. Radcliffe explained. "I ought to take him back to the Tower. Would you like to walk part of the way back with me? That is, if have you the time."

"Certainly. I have all the time in the world. People are used to me taking long walks." Actually, she realized that was only true when she was at home. She tended not to ramble as widely here, where she did not yet know the countryside.

Any time now, someone might wonder where Willa was. Miss Hadfield might have returned from her errands; her mother might have noticed her absence. Despite that, she did not turn back. Instead, she walked on by Mr. Radcliffe's side, trying to ignore the angry rumble of the waves.

"Is your aunt any better today?" she asked.

He shrugged. "A little, I think. She seems to be past the worst of the sickness, but she is not recovering as quickly as we hoped. It will probably be some time before she resumes her usual responsibilities." He frowned thoughtfully. "It is strange that no one else was sick."

"Oh, but your aunt was not the only one! My cousin Sarah— Mrs. Trimmer—had an upset stomach after the picnic. But she recovered in a day or two, and no one else in our family sickened. You didn't know?"

"No. I thought Aunt Faith was the only one." A wrinkle formed between his brows as he stared into the distance.

Willa, recognizing the signs of someone lost in thought, allowed him the silence to think. When they reached the outcropping of rock that marked the end of Newell Beach, he gestured to the rough trail that wound up the sloping side of the cliffs.

"This path is much faster than the stairs on the other side of the cover, but not nearly as easy. Do you think you can scramble up to the top of the cliffs, Lady Wilhelmina? Or would you rather turn back?"

Cato had run ahead and was already halfway up the slope. He looked back over his shoulder, as if wondering why they hadn't followed him yet.

She studied the rough slope. It really wasn't that steep, and she was wearing her sturdiest half boots. "I do not need to turn back. Let us keep walking."

At the back of her mind, a little voice whispered that the longer she spent in Mr. Radcliffe's company, the greater the potential scandal. But they had never really discussed his plan to try reading by the ocean. She wanted to hear more about that.

She did not really have to scramble to get to the top, but the ascent did take most of her attention and all of her breath. Neither of them spoke until they reached the cliff. Then she drew a deep breath.

Mr. Radcliffe broke the silence. "I have been thinking about that stomach upset. I wonder if it could have been something your cousin and my aunt both ate?"

Willa considered that, then shook her head. "We all ate the same foods. If anything tainted or foul was served that day, we all should have gotten sick."

"Maybe." He sounded doubtful, though, so Willa was not surprised when he continued on to say, "In my experience, different people may react in different ways to the same food. And it can change over time. There are many foods my grandfather used to love that now give him indigestion. There are foods that I can't swallow because they feel so awful in my mouth. And my father had a friend who died while eating lobster."

"Lobster?" she repeated, horrified. "I never knew lobster could be dangerous." She loved lobster patties.

"That's my point," he said. "It was dangerous for Mr. Hampton, but not for anyone else at the table."

Willa nodded. "I see. You are suggesting that whatever made Miss Marlowe and Cousin Sarah sick might have been perfectly safe for everyone else." Certainly, *she* had felt no ill effects from anything she'd eaten at the picnic.

"Yes, especially since they are older than you or me, or even Miss Hadfield. Maybe our youth protected us."

"You could be right," she admitted. Willa's mother was only

a little younger than Ben's aunt, but who knew whether that really made a difference? They would probably never know for sure what had made Miss Marlowe so sick.

After that, they walked in silence. Mr. Radcliffe took the gravel trail that led to Castle Rock Point. Willa followed him, though she kept her head stiffly directed away from the ocean.

Maybe Mr. Radcliffe was right that she ought to work on overcoming her phobia. It seemed a pity that she could not enjoy a trip to the seaside the way everyone else did. Was she to spend the rest of her life avoiding beaches and bathing machines? She did regret that she could not fully appreciate the scenery on today's walk. The view from the cliffs would have been splendid if not for her phobia.

The cold splash of a raindrop heralded the fulfillment of Phoebe's prediction. Willa was indeed caught in the rain, nearly a mile from Cousin Sarah's house. She opened her umbrella, wondering whether she should offer to share it with Mr. Radcliffe.

Before she could ask, Mr. Radcliffe interrupted the silence. "Do the stars bother you the same way?"

The question came out of nowhere, stopping Willa in her tracks. "The stars? Do they bother me the same way as what?"

"Do the heights of the heavens bother you the way the depths of the ocean do?" He waved a hand towards the restless waters below the cliff. "I happened to remember a night when I was a boy, and my tutor took me out to study the constellations. We lay down on blankets and looked up, and. . ." He caught her gaze and held it.

"And?" she prompted. Why, she wondered, had Miss Hadfield never thought to take her out at night for an astronomy lesson? Naturally, Willa had seen the stars at night, even as a child, but she had never *studied* them.

He drew a deep breath, then said the rest of it in a rush. "I looked up at the stars and thought about how the world was turning on its axis orbiting the sun, and it made me feel as if the rotation might spin me off into the depths of space. There was nothing between me and the stars but miles and miles of space, and the immensity of the heavens terrified me. Only for a moment, but I remember it very clearly."

They stared at each other. Willa had no idea what her companion was thinking, but she felt amazed that he'd shared such a memory with her. In her experience, most gentlemen did not like admitting to having been afraid of anything.

He lowered his eyes and kicked at the gravel in front of him. "Anyway, I wondered if your fear of the ocean were a little like that."

"Yes, it does sound similar." The breath she drew felt weighted with significance. "You are the only person I have ever met who understood."

Their eyes met as she marveled over the unexpected connection. No one had ever understood her fear of the ocean; most people didn't even *try* to understand. Mr. Radcliffe must be the one man out of a million who not only understood but had experienced something similar to her dread of the ocean's depths.

She would have to be a fool to let such a precious discovery get away from her.

Chapter Seventeen

Y*OU ARE THE only person I have ever met who understood.* Her words revolved in Ben's head, rising like bubbles in champagne.

Ben thoroughly understood the experience of being misunderstood, of being an anomalous segment that clashed with the rest of the pattern. The times when he encountered the opposite situation—when he knew, deep in his bones, that someone else shared and understood his experience—were both rare and precious. He wanted to store this moment in his memory so he could treasure it forever.

Unfortunately, Wordsworth was right when he wrote, "The world is too much with us." The sweet rapport Ben felt with Lady Wilhelmina vanished when a strident voice hailed him from farther up the path.

"Master Benjamin? Did you know that your aunt is looking for you? Why are you standing out here in the rain?"

Rain? It wasn't—oh! When he tipped his head up to look at the sky, a raindrop fell into his eye. It *was* raining. For some reason, he hadn't even noticed. Now that he paid attention to his surroundings again, he saw that Lady Wilhelmina had already opened an umbrella. When had that happened?

"Master Benjamin?" the footman called again.

"I will be with you shortly! Tell my aunt not to worry!" Ben called back.

"I suppose this is where we part," Lady Wilhemina suggested.

Ben peered up at the sky again. Dark clouds laden with rain stretched as far as the eye could see. "You had better not walk home in this rain. I will have our coachman drive you back into town."

The corners of her mouth lifted, and she looked relieved. "I would appreciate that."

He hurried them into the house. The French doors opening out of the library were closest, so he headed there rather than going all the way around to the formal front entrance.

Then disaster struck. Ben opened the door for his guest and gestured her into the library. When he stepped in after her, he saw, to his dismay, that the room was already occupied. His grandfather sat by the fire, accompanied by Mr. Traherne, the vicar. Both men held brandy glasses in their hands and wore matching expressions of surprise.

Grandfather Marlowe rose to a belated stand. "Good morning, Lady Wilhelmina. I was not aware that you had come to call. Is Mrs. Trimmer with you?"

Rosy pink color spread across her cheeks. "No, I am alone." She shot a nervous glance at Ben, though he could not tell what he she meant to communicate. "I mean, I went for my morning walk and happened to meet Mr. Radcliffe. I sought shelter here because of the rain."

"Yes, I thought I would have Jamison drive her back to her cousin's house," Ben explained. "So she would not have to walk back to town in the rain." That was a perfectly reasonable proposition. Why, then, did his grandfather look so grim?

"Of course we will send your friend home in a carriage." Grandfather's frown faded as he addressed Lady Wilhelmina herself. "In the meantime, why don't you come to the drawing room and take a cup of tea to warm you up, my lady?"

She directed another one of those nervous glances at Ben, as if she expected him to help her out. Between her concern and his grandfather's glowering, Ben felt under siege. Why couldn't people simply ask for what they wanted, or say exactly what they wanted, instead of expecting him to interpret cryptic looks or furtive glances?

Grandfather's voice softened as he coaxed Lady Wilhelmina into accepting the invitation. "It will take Jamison time to harness the horses. You might as well come in and warm yourself."

After that, everything went smoothly, and Ben wondered if he had imagined the frown on his grandfather's face. But as soon as the coach pulled away, his grandfather's affability vanished.

He cleared his throat to get Ben's attention. "We had better sit down in the library and talk, Benjamin." He used precisely the tone he had used back when Ben was a child who had gotten into trouble.

But Ben was not a child by any definition of the term. He was a grown man. Other men his age kept chambers in London, or lived at the Inns of Court, and got into all manner of mischief without being scolded as if they were twelve rather than two-and-twenty.

He would have to remind his grandfather of that, he decided. As he followed Grandfather Marlowe into the library, he prepared a mental list of bullet points to use in his argument.

Ben's grandfather did not give him a chance to make an argument. As soon as he settled back into the most comfortable chair, he attacked. "Benjamin Radcliffe, do you expect me to believe that story of you encountering Lady Wilhelmina by accident?" He shook his head. "I thought it was odd that you chose to walk on Newell Beach rather than the Cove this morning. You went there to meet her, didn't you?"

Reduced to speechlessness, Ben opened and closed his mouth like a hungry goldfish.

His grandfather raised his eyebrows. "You cannot deny it, can you? You really arranged a secret rendezvous with a respectable young lady?"

Ben flinched. "You are making it sound far worse than it

really was. Lady Wilhelmina and I met up to take a walk together. There is nothing scandalous about walking along a public beach with a young lady, is there?" He refrained from mentioning that part of their walk had taken place on private property.

"Even on a public beach, it would be better to have a chaperone accompany you," his grandfather insisted. "But the walk itself is not my real objection. What concerns me is how secretive you were. Did Lady Wilhelmina's family know she was meeting up with you?"

Ben's mouth hung ajar. "I... don't know," he admitted. "Probably not." If they'd known she intended to meet Ben, they would almost certainly have sent someone to accompany her.

"As I thought." Grandfather Marlowe shook his head slowly. "Benjamin, when a man has honorable intentions towards a woman, he does not hide his meetings with her."

Ben leapt to his feet. Hot anger ran through his veins, sending a flush to his face. "I assure you, I have no dishonorable intentions towards Lady Wilhelmina or any other lady!" He clenched his hands.

His grandfather looked taken aback, but he rallied quickly. "You are not acting honorably by her. If anyone discovers that you arranged a clandestine meeting with her, her good name would be dragged through the mud. Such actions can ruin a young lady. For all you know, you may have already destroyed Lady Wilhelmina's reputation."

He tightened his fists, driving his nails into his palms. "Not if I marry her!" he retorted. "A betrothed couple is allowed to take walks alone." At least, he thought they were. But he often struggled to understand the niceties of such social regulations.

"Are you betrothed to her, then?" This time, there was a distinctively skeptical cast to Grandfather's arched eyebrows. "Because if so, my felicitations. If not, then I stand by everything I have already said, and I suggest you avoid any further contact with the young lady."

Ben blinked and slowly relaxed his hands. Those were his only options? Become betrothed to Lady Wilhelmina, or end their friendship merely to preserve her reputation?

It took him only a moment to decide. Friendship had never come easily to Ben. Too often he misunderstood other people, or they misunderstood him. He could not bear to abandon a promising friendship because of potential scandal.

"We are not betrothed yet," he admitted. "But I am going to propose to her today. Right now, in fact. Will that make you happy, sir?"

"Yes." His grandfather scanned Ben from head to foot. "You may wish to change your clothing first. And for goodness' sake, comb your hair!"

Ben bit back an angry retort. How humiliating it was to be treated like a child even when he was on the verge of offering his hand in marriage to a woman! Would his family ever recognize his maturity?

Worst of all, when he looked at himself in the mirror, he saw that his grandfather was right. He did look a right mess. He would have preferred to rush off and pop the question right away, before he lost his nerve, but he conceded that he ought to appear his best on such an important occasion.

Though he usually walked into town, the steady rain prevented that today. Fortunately, he dressed himself in time to catch Jamison before the horses were unhitched. Jamison was probably not happy about turning the carriage around and heading right back into Newell, but he made no outward complaint.

Ben didn't remember the gift he'd set aside for Lady Wilhelmina until he climbed into the carriage. "Wait a moment," he called to the coachman. "I have to fetch something."

He'd fashioned the sea glass trinket despite his doubts about whether it would be an appropriate gift for a gentleman to give a lady. No such doubts need trouble him now. If she accepted his proposal, no one would think it untoward for him to shower his betrothed with gifts.

He had no intention of spending a king's ransom on precious gems. The Radcliffe family owned an heirloom set of pearls for formal events, and amethysts for day wear. That ought to be enough jewelry even for an earl's daughter—oughtn't it?

Now that he thought about, he had no idea how much jewelry a woman from the aristocracy might wear. All of *his* relatives belonged to the gentry. What if the Selwyn family objected to him on that account? His stomach lurched as he realized that betrothal and matrimony might turn out to be more complicated than he'd anticipated.

Too late to back out now! He had told his grandfather he was going to make an offer to Lady Wilhelmina. Time to make good on that promise. He retrieved a little wooden box from his bedroom, returned to the carriage, and ordered Jamison to drive on.

For all he knew, he might be riding towards failure. Even so, he might as well get the failure over with so he could move on.

Chapter Eighteen

WILLA'S MOTHER WAS deep into a long harangue when the maid tapped at the bedroom door to announce that someone had called for Willa. The housemaid neglected to say who had called, leaving Willa to speculate wildly.

Lady Inglewhite sighed. "I suppose you had better go see to your guest. But I hope that in the future you behave more circumspectly. You know better than to ramble across the countryside with a young man!"

"Yes, Mama. I will make certain it never happens again." Willa resisted the temptation to cross her fingers behind her back. Privately, she resolved to do a better job of hiding any future indiscretions—assuming there were any.

Her mother frowned. Maybe she'd heard Willa's unspoken reservations. "Remember, I expect you to set a good example for your sister. Phoebe looks to you for guidance on how to behave like a well-bred young lady, you know."

"Yes, Mama, I know." Willa had heard this line before. *Many* times before. Strange how important her example supposedly was to Phoebe. Willa had never had an older sister to emulate, yet she turned out just fine, hadn't she? Apart from the rambling-cross-country-without-a-chaperone problem, that was.

In any case, it was a relief to leave her mother's scolding behind to greet her caller. She should have been surprised when she opened the door to the parlor and found Mr. Radcliffe. But somehow, she was not surprised. Who else could it have been? She had become acquainted with some of Cousin Sarah's friends and neighbors, but none of them would have specifically asked for *her* when they called.

Mr. Radcliffe stood beside the empty fireplace, his hands clasped behind his back. He had replaced his dark-blue tailcoat with a hunter-green one, and his plain waistcoat had given way to one with golden embroidery.

He inclined his head to her. "Lady Wilhelmina, I am glad to see that you made it home safely."

She struggled to suppress the grin that tugged at the corners of her mouth. It was not likely that anything would threaten her safety on the short carriage ride back from Marlowe Tower.

A line formed between his brows. "Did I say something funny?"

She heard a hint of real anxiety in his voice, so she hastened to reassure him. "No, Mr. Radcliffe. I amused myself by wondering if you had come all this way to just to make certain I arrived home in one piece."

"Ah, I see." He stared down at the floor as if he had never before seen a carpet from Turkey. "No, I did not call merely to make certain you arrived safely."

"I thought not." Willa used her softest, gentlest voice, because she had not seen Mr. Radcliffe this nervous for ages. Over the last few weeks, he had grown more comfortable in her company. So it seemed, at least. But now all of that ease was gone. "What does bring you here today, Mr. Radcliffe?"

He lifted his eyes back to her face. "I wish you would call me Ben! It sounds very strange to hear *Mister* on your lips."

She drew in a sharp breath. How on earth was she supposed to respond to that? If he had been a girl—the B.R. she had once imagined—they might have been on first-name terms by now. Calling a gentleman by his first name, though, was an entirely different matter.

"Not that I was thinking about your lips!" he hastily clarified. A flush slowly rose up his whole face, all the way to the tips of his ears. "I only meant that you could call me by my given name. If you wanted. But perhaps you don't want to."

He closed his eyes and scrubbed his face with one hand. "I am getting this all wrong. What if we pretended the last five minutes never happened?"

"Very well." Uncle Rowland had once told Willa, "When in doubt, tell a joke." She doubted that tip was useful in all situations, but it might work well here. If she could get Mr. Radcliffe to smile, maybe he would not feel so anxious.

Willa walked backwards to the door, then stepped into the room and dropped a curtsey, as if she had only just arrived. "Good afternoon, Mr. Radcliffe. What a pleasure to see you again so soon!"

A grin slowly spread across his face. For a moment he looked like he was going to argue, but then he began to play along. "I am glad to see that you arrived home safely, Lady Wilhelmina. I beg the favor of a few minutes of conversation with you. I have come to speak to you on a most important subject."

A jolt of foreboding, as potent and exhilarating as electricity, made Willa's heart turn a somersault. She could only think of one subject important enough to demand such formal language. It would explain Mr. Radcliffe's nervousness, too.

He was no longer the only one troubled by nerves. Willa licked her lips. "Yes, Mr. Radcliffe? What did you wish to say to me?"

"It is a simple question, really." He stood soldier-straight, still clasping his hands behind his back. "I wondered if you would do me the very great honor of becoming my wife." He sounded as if he were reading the words off a script.

"You have taken me by surprise, sir. I had not realized that, um. . ." Willa pulled herself up short. What on earth was she *saying*? His proposal was not *entirely* a surprise. After their last few encounters, she had suspected that Mr. Radcliffe's interest in her might be of a romantic nature.

She tried again. "I had not expected you to speak to me on this subject yet. I am not certain how to answer you." That was more honest.

The doubtful crease returned to his forehead. "Would you prefer I wait and ask again later? There is no real rush. I only thought that being betrothed might make some things easier for us."

Confused, Willa asked, "What do you mean, 'easier'?" She suspected planning a wedding and preparing for a life together took a great deal of work.

"I mean that it would be easier to find ways of meeting," he explained. "Engaged couples are usually given more freedom to interact, aren't they? I doubt anyone would complain about us taking a walk by the beach without a chaperone if we were formally betrothed."

"Oh." He had a point. A good one, in fact.

To be sure, he assumed that Willa *wanted* to take walks alone with him, but his assumption was correct. She would like to be able to spend time alone with Mr. Radcliffe. How could a young lady get to know a gentleman if she only met him in the company of others?

"Why don't you take a seat?" Willa suggested. "I would like a moment to think this over, if you don't mind." A spot of tea would not go amiss, either.

While Mr. Radcliffe—Benjamin?—settled in a stiff wooden armchair, Willa rang for the maid and instructed her to bring tea and biscuits. "Lavender biscuits, if we have them," she qualified.

A smile flitted across her face as she remembered Ben's attempt to "train" her using those biscuits. Then her heart sank. Was *that* what this sudden proposal was all about?

She settled on the sofa, keeping some distance between her and her suitor. "You may be right that becoming engaged would give us more freedom. But what do we need that freedom for? Are you proposing to me only so we can continue your experiment?"

"Experiment?" He looked startled.

"I mean the attempt to, ah, help me overcome my fear of the ocean by associating it with something I like." They never had gotten to try his plan of reading G.W. Kirkland on the beach. Willa had doubts about whether it would work, but it was at least an interesting idea.

The look of confusion left his face. "Oh! Well, it did occur to me that we might have more success with that project if we were allowed to spend more time together. But that isn't the only reason." He rubbed his hands over the knees of his trousers. "I thought we suited each other well. That is, I thought we might understand each other. . . at least, better than might be the case with other people."

Willa nodded. "That is probably true." But was that *enough*? He had said nothing about affection. She cleared her throat before bringing up that weighty issue. "Our grandparents' generation may have believed respect to be an adequate foundation for a marriage, but I have always ascribed to the view that one should never marry without love."

"Oh." He looked disappointed. "Do you mean that you do not love me enough to marry me?"

The question took Willa by surprise, though she ought to have anticipated it. "I am not sure how to answer that," she admitted. "I am not sure what being in love feels like."

He simply nodded. "Precisely. If one has never been in love, how is one supposed to recognize it?" He drew a deep breath. "But I like you, Lady Wilhelmina. And I-I think you are very beautiful." A faint blush rose along his cheekbones. "I do not know whether I love you, but I think I could."

Willa had always assumed that when her future husband proposed to her, something special would happen. She had expected to feel fireworks or champagne bubbles— metaphorically, of course. Or perhaps she would go weak in her knees.

But, though she was sitting down, her knees felt no different than usual. No rockets burst into fireworks in her heart, nor did she feel the least bit tipsy.

On the other hand, her heart pounded as if she had been running, and a pleasant warmth flushed her body. She felt as if she stood on the edge of a precipice nearly as deep as the ocean itself.

But the decision before her did not threaten her with an endless fall into darkness. If she took a step forward into the unknown, someone or something would keep her from falling. For some reason, she felt certain of that.

She squeezed her hands together. "I do not know if I love you yet, either. But I think I could. And I would like to try."

He rose from his chair and approached her slowly, as if he feared she might startle and bolt, like a frightened horse. Willa rose to her feet. When Mr. Radcliffe reached her, he took her hands in his. Neither of them of them wore gloves, so his bare skin brushed against hers, sparking another unexpected flutter of her heart.

"Will you marry me, then?" His cool green eyes held her gaze. She could not have looked away if she wanted to.

Fortunately, she did not want to look away.

She swallowed before answering. She did have one stipulation, and she was not at all certain how he would respond to it. Though she paused only a moment, her hesitation put a frown back on Mr. Radcliffe's face. "I will accept your offer, with one condition."

His frown deepened. "Yes? What condition?" His voice fairly crackled with apprehension.

"If either of us comes to regret the betrothal, or have serious doubts, then we will break the engagement. We should both be free to change our minds."

Mr. Radcliffe opened his mouth to protest, but she hushed him with a raised finger. She would like to have silenced him with a fingertip pressed against his lips, but she had no idea whether he would welcome such a touch.

"I know that a gentleman is never supposed to break an engagement," she said. "That privilege belongs to the lady. But in this case, since neither of us are certain of the depth of our affections, I think we ought to leave room in case. . . in case either of us finds that we have mistaken our feelings."

The corners of his mouth turned down. He still looked like he wanted to protest.

Willa drew a deep breath and stated her caveat more plainly. "If you come to realize that you do not love me, or if for any other reason you want out of the engagement, you have only to ask. And you must promise me that you *will* ask if you have second thoughts. I do not want to trap you into a loveless marriage."

"I see." He gently squeezed her hand. "That is a reasonable condition, my lady. I promise to tell you if I should change my mind or my feelings. Naturally, the same applies to you. You must not hesitate to tell me if you wish to end the engagement. I would never want you to enter into an unwanted marriage, either."

Willa released a tiny sigh. She'd been afraid he might protest her condition. It did, after all, run counter to the usual rules. But Mr. Radcliffe seemed too sensible to mistake etiquette for ethics, the way some people did.

She cleared her throat. "One more thing. . ."

"Yes?" he asked anxiously.

She lowered her eyes, feeling unexpectedly bashful. "You do not need to call me 'my lady,' or 'Lady Wilhelmina.' If you are my intended, you should call me by my given name. In fact, I think you ought to call me *Willa*, as everyone else does." Everyone whom she loved, that is.

A broad smile banished the worry line from his forehead. "Only if you call me Ben. And—oh, wait! I should give you this."

He fumbled in his pocket, finally pulling out a small wooden box. Willa accepted it gingerly, privately hoping it was not something expensive. She hated to think he might have spent a fortune on a gift without even knowing if she would accept it.

When she opened the box, though, she broke into a delighted smile. "That bit of sea glass! You did turn it into a pendant! How pretty!"

And how thoughtful. She'd made the comment about turning the sea glass into jewelry weeks ago. He had not only listened but remembered what she said.

She lifted the pendant out of the box. It was already attached to a silver chain, but the clasp proved difficult to work.

Willa glanced up at her new fiancé. "Will you help me put this on?"

He nodded, and she turned her back so that he could fasten the necklace.

Many times in the past, a maid had helped her with a garment, a ribbon, or a piece of jewelry, but this felt far more intimate. Every hair on the back of Willa's neck stood up when Ben's fingers brushed against the sensitive skin on her nape. She heard him catch his breath. Did he feel it, too?

When he finished, she turned to face him. "Thank you," she breathed.

She half expected him to move away, because he stood much closer than was proper. From here, she saw that his pupils had widened, swallowing up most of the green in his eyes. His Adam's apple moved as he gulped.

"Now I would like to ask a request of my own, if I may?" His voice wavered.

"Of course!" What was he so nervous about?

"I would like to kiss you." Ben's hoarse whisper sent a delicious shiver down Willa's spine. "May I?"

Now her knees really did feel weak, but she did not hesitate to answer, "You may."

He stepped even closer to her—so close that she felt the warmth of his body through her silk gown—and slipped one arm around her waist, resting his hand on the small of her back. When he cupped her face with his other hand, heat rolled from her blushing face down her whole body, all the way to the tips of her toes.

Willa tipped her face up and waited, heart racing, as her new fiancé slanted his mouth down. At first, he brushed his lips lightly against hers. Then he teased her lips apart, focusing on her bottom lip.

What, exactly, was *she* supposed to do? She would have asked for instructions, but her mouth was currently occupied.

She shivered when his teeth gently scraped against her lip. She'd had no idea people used their teeth when they kissed, but the sensation wasn't unpleasant—merely unexpected.

Nor did she expect the soft creak of the door hinge or the startled gasp that followed. She stumbled backwards in her haste to get away from Ben, realizing too late that doing so made her look more guilty. So did the blush filling her face, but she could do nothing to stop that.

"Very sorry, miss." The housemaid deposited the tea tray on an end table, then backed out of the room.

"Maybe I should go speak to my mother?" Willa suggested. Better for her mother to learn of the engagement from Willa than from the servants' gossiping.

"I think I should do it," Ben countered. "I suppose I should also write to your guardian. Er, assuming you have one?"

Willa nodded. "My uncle Richard is my guardian. The current Lord Inglewhite, I mean. If you wish to write a note for him, my mother can enclose it in one of her letters. That way she can introduce you to him properly."

"Very well. I will speak to her now." He lifted her hand to his lips and brushed a kiss against it. Then he hurried out of the room.

Willa sank down onto the sofa. Had she really just accepted a proposal of marriage? Goodness! There were few decisions more important for a woman than the choice of a husband. A woman's future, her quality of life, and even her safety depended on making a good choice.

Given all that, Willa expected to feel anxious or doubtful about her answer. Instead, she felt only a quiet joy, as fragile as a soap bubble. She closed her eyes and treasured the moment.

No, she had no fears for the future. What could go wrong?

Chapter Nineteen

THE FIRST FEW days of his betrothal were among the happiest Ben could remember. Nearly every day, he and Willa met. Either he called at Mrs. Trimmer's house in Newell, or he and Willa met for an afternoon walk on the Marlowe grounds.

Aunt Faith and Grandfather Marlowe both approved of Ben's intended, but not of the way he treated her. When Willa and Lady Inglewhite dined at the Tower one evening, Aunt Faith watched the sweethearts, her brow furrowed in perplexity.

After the Selwyn ladies left, Ben's aunt scolded him. "Ben, I don't understand why you did nothing but sit in silence with Lady Wilhelmina all evening. I know you enjoy reading, but you could read a book any time you want. Why didn't you spend your time conversing with her? Making her feel welcome?"

Grandfather Marlowe chimed in with his agreement. "Yes, indeed. You should be spending this time getting to know her better. You will have the rest of your life to read books."

"I *am* getting to know her," Ben insisted. "Reading in a room with Willa is different than reading alone." Her presence in a room added an ineffable quality to the experience. It made Ben happier, though he could not explain why.

"I hope, for your sake, she feels the same way." His aunt's voice sounded tart, but a faint smile lurked in the corners of her mouth.

Seeing that smile, Ben turned the conversation to his advantage. "You can see how well suited we are," he pointed out. "*She* made no complaint about how we spent the evening." If she did not mind quietly reading at his side, why should anyone else mind?

"I do not understand the young people of this generation." Grandfather Marlowe shook his head, though he, too, now looked amused rather than angry. "But I suppose there are worse things the two of you might do."

Ben wondered what his family would have thought if they had known the true purpose of the afternoon walks he and Willa often took together. They inevitably went towards Castle Rock Point. There, they sat on the wrought-iron bench, and Ben read aloud from *Terror at Carringford Park* while Willa worked on her embroidery.

Ben's plan was to read the first volume of the novel up on the point, far above the waves. When they reached the second volume, they would walk down to the beach, starting out closer to the cliffs and gradually moving out towards the water. That was very similar to what his father had done with his hunting dog. What worked for dogs ought to work even better for people, who were more intelligent than dogs. Or so Ben reasoned.

As for the third volume of the novel. . . he secretly hoped that by then, Willa would feel comfortable enough to sit in a boat. Not a little dinghy, of course, but something a bit larger. It was rather a pity Ben did not know anyone who owned a yacht, but there were certainly boats enough to be found in Newell.

They were within two chapters of the end of the first volume when an unexpected visitor disturbed the peace at Marlowe Tower. Ben came back from a ramble with Cato to find that, this time, two of his cousins had arrived for an unannounced visit. Marlowe Milllington had returned, bringing his older sister with him.

Almeria beamed at Ben when he walked into the drawing room. "Ben! I hear that you have been felled by Cupid's arrow at last. My felicitations on your betrothal!"

He flinched. Whereas Marlowe oozed soft-spoken charm, Almeria's bold voice carried from one end of the house to another. This trait would have been useful if she had been a schoolmistress; she could have easily called a class to attention without employing a bell. Unfortunately, her voice had always grated on Ben's ears.

"Thank you," he said, hoping no one had noticed his initial recoil. "I am very happy about the betrothal."

"I should think so, marrying an earl's daughter! How on earth did you land such a catch, Ben?" Marlowe laughed, as if it were nothing but a witticism, but it carried the usual bitter sting.

Ben shrugged, pretending he didn't mind his cousin's discourtesy. After all, it was nothing new. "I am indeed very fortunate." He forced a perfunctory smile to his lips, then changed the subject. "What brings the two of you to Dorset?" He wouldn't put it past Marlowe to travel all this way purely for the purpose of harassing Ben.

Almeria put a hand over her heart. "We have all been so very concerned about Aunt Faith. Our mother thought we ought to come see for ourselves how she did."

"She has recovered quite well," Ben assured them. Aunt Faith did complain of a few lingering stomach pains, but apart from that, she seemed to be enjoying her usual health. "You can carry a good report back to your mother when you return to Winchester." He hoped that would be soon.

"And, of course, Almeria would like to meet Miss Selwyn," Marlowe put in.

"Lady Wilhelmina, you mean," Ben gently corrected. The system of aristocratic ranks and titles seemed rather silly to Ben, but he could not stand to hear Willa spoken of with disrespect.

"Of course, of course. I meant no offense." The familiar sneer on Marlowe's face undermined his apology. He knew perfectly well how to address the daughter of an earl, so he must have omitted the title to irritate Ben.

Ben worried about how his cousins might behave when face-to-face with Willa, but when Willa next dined with them, Marlowe and Almeria were on their best behavior—at least when talking to *her*.

Willa wore the same white evening gown she had worn the first time she dined at Marlowe Tower, but this time, she also wore the sea glass pendant Ben had given her. When it glinted in the candlelight, it was almost as bright as her azure eyes. The jewelry could not have looked so lovely on anyone else in the world, Ben decided.

Before dinner began, Almeria chatted with Willa about fashion, travel, and resort towns. Somehow, Almeria sounded sophisticated and worldly, though Ben knew for a fact that she'd spent most of her life in a quiet cathedral town.

Naturally, Marlowe kept up his usual practice of slipping jibes and sneers at Ben whenever he could, but he only did so when the women couldn't hear him. Altogether, the evening could have been much worse.

Even so, by the time dinner ended, Ben felt exhausted. He sat in a quiet corner with a book, though the light was not good enough for reading. He did not particularly want to read this treatise on chemistry, anyway. He merely wielded it as a shield to deflect unwanted conversation.

When he did listen in on the conversations around him, he overheard Almeria asking his aunt a series of disconnected questions—about what kind of tea she drank, whether she took sugar in it, and did Grandfather Marlowe still have a sweet tooth?

Grandfather answered the last question for himself. "Too many foods disagree with me these days! I do not eat cakes and cookies anymore, though I do still take sugar with my tea."

Ben was not surprised when Willa drifted over to his side of the room shortly after that. "Why on earth is Almeria talking so much about food?" he asked.

She shrugged. "Maybe she's hungry. Maybe she means to ask your grandfather to visit her home, and she wants to know what food to serve."

"She lives with her mother still," Ben explained, "and I don't think their house is big enough for entertaining guests." He could be wrong about that, though. It had been years since he'd visited his Millington relatives in their own home.

"Do *you* take sugar in your tea?" A teasing glint shone from Willa's eyes.

Ben smiled. Unlike Marlowe's jibes, Willa's gentle teasing always left him feeling warmer. "No, but when I drink chocolate, I take it with sugar. When it is unsweetened, it is too bitter for me."

"I like chocolate either way." Willa covered a dainty yawn. Then she glanced across the room to where her mother sat in conversation with Ben's grandfather.

Ben was not surprised that the Selwyn ladies soon departed. Sadly, he did not see the last of Almeria and Marlowe for a few more days. Finally, they returned to Winchester, leaving Ben glad to see the back of them. With any luck, it would be months before he'd have to tolerate Marlowe's snide little comments again.

WITH HIS MILLINGTON cousins gone, Ben hoped life would return to normal. More accurately, to the new normal that included Willa. But the very day after they left, a new visitor arrived.

Ben's aunt joined him at the window to watch a traveling chariot pull up in front of the Tower. It bore a familiar coat of arms—familiar, in this case, meaning the Radcliffe coat of arms.

Ben exchanged puzzled glances with his aunt. "Were you expecting more visitors?" He'd heard nothing from his parents about a visit to Dorset.

"No, but—" She paused as a footman opened the carriage door.

A man nearly as tall and lean as Ben stepped out of the carriage. His brown hair, once darker than Ben's, was now dusted with gray at the temples. Ben knew that figure as well as he knew his own form. It was his father, Sir Lewis Radcliffe.

"I suspect your father wishes to speak to you about your betrothal," his aunt predicted.

Ben sucked in his breath, suddenly worried. "You don't think he objects to the engagement, do you?" Most people would think Ben was marrying above himself, given Willa's rank. If *her* family had no objections, what grounds for objection could Ben's family have?

He did not learn the answer to that until after dinner. Tonight, Grandfather Marlowe disappeared into his study as soon as Aunt Faith withdrew from the dining room. Ben and his father were left alone with their wineglasses. He wondered if his father had planned it that way.

"Now, Benjamin," his father said, "let us have a comfortable chat about this betrothal of yours."

Benjamin? Normally, his father called him "Ben," like everyone else. The use of his full name was not a good sign.

Knowing he would need all his wits about him, Ben put down his glass of port. His father's "comfortable chats" sometimes turned out to be grueling interrogations.

He eyed his father warily. "What would you like to know? I believe the Selwyn family's solicitor has already contacted Williamson about settlements, so he will know the financial details better than I do."

Ben had been rather shocked when he learned how large Lady Wilhelmina's dowry was, but that money would all be settled on her future children. Still, it was nice to know that their newlywed income would not depend solely on Ben's allowance.

"I am not concerned about settlements, Benjamin. I am wondering why you wish to marry at such a young age. What made you rush into a betrothal?"

Ben's eyes widened. He had not expected this line of inquiry.

"I wish to marry because I found someone with whom I wanted to spend my life." It wasn't a particularly good answer, but he didn't think the question deserved a better one. "Why else would anyone want to get married?"

Sir Lewis frowned. "You have years yet before you need worry about choosing a wife or setting up your nursery. You would do better to spend some time sowing your wild oats in London. You would pick up some Town-bronze, and you might make useful acquaintances."

On second thought, Ben might need the fortification of alcohol after all. He took a healthy gulp of port and tried not to think too deeply about what his father meant by "sowing wild oats."

"I have no desire to spend a fortune in gaming hells or set up a mistress," he said bluntly.

His father shook his head. "Of course we don't want you gambling away the family coffers! As for a mistress, do you have any idea how expensive a high-flyer is?"

Ben narrowed his eyes. How did his father know how much it cost to keep a mistress? He opened his mouth to ask, but Sir Lewis did not give him the chance.

"Nevertheless, there are other means of gaining experience in, ah, adult life." Sir Lewis stared into his wineglass rather than look Ben in the face. "I would like to see you get your feet wet a little before you take the plunge into matrimony." He took a gulp of wine, evidently feeling the awkwardness of this conversation every bit as much as Ben.

Starting to get lost in his father's metaphors, Ben decided to get straight to the point. "If you mean to suggest that I should visit a brothel in order to lose my virginity, I can assure you I have already done that." Ben had visited Schools of Venus a handful of times, usually under pressure from acquaintances at Cambridge. He had mixed feelings about those experiences, but he could not deny that they'd been instructive.

His father sputtered. He covered his mouth, but not quickly enough to prevent wine from spraying onto the table. His ears turned red, too. Evidently, Ben's bluntness made him uncomfortable. Good! Ben saw no reason to keep all the awkwardness of this conversation to himself.

"I did not mean *only* that," Sir Lewis clarified. "Although that is certainly one of the experiences I had in mind. My point is that a man can satisfy his physical desires in many different ways. Being tired of celibacy is hardly reason enough to enter into a permanent—"

Ben interrupted his father before the conversation could get any more mortifying. "I think you are laboring under a misconception, sir. I did not propose to Lady Wilhelmina because I was desperate to, er, satisfy my physical desires." He did look forward to going to bed with his new wife, but he had absolutely no desire to discuss *that* with his father.

He paused only to catch his breath, not wanting to give his father time to interrupt. "I proposed to Lady Wilhelmina because I have enjoyed my friendship with her, and I thought our betrothal—and subsequent marriage—would foster the development of our friendship."

His father drew his brows down, but he looked confused rather than unhappy. "Benjamin, people do not marry their friends."

"*I* do." Ben took another sip of port. "At least, I plan to marry this particular friend. I would not marry any of my other friends." For many reasons, not least because he'd never wanted to kiss any of his other friends. Fortified by wine, he turned the tables. "Father, have you any reason to believe Lady Wilhelmina would not be a good match for me?"

His father lowered his gaze. "No," he admitted. "So far as her connections and situation in life go, it is an excellent match. Your mother and I would never have expected you to marry into the aristocracy. If you were a few years older, I would not have the least objection."

"I am of age," Ben reminded him. "And I don't see why I should have to wait years to get married if I have already found the person I want to marry."

Sir Lewis turned his wineglass around in his hand, apparently mesmerized by the swirl of the tawny port. "Fair enough," he grudgingly responded. "What if you agreed to wait one year to marry?"

Ben's eyes widened. *A year?* Most engagements lasted no more than a few months! "That would make sense if I were still a minor. But I am not. As for Lady Wilhelmina. . . surely you don't think *she* is too young to marry?" She was only a couple of years younger than Ben.

His father put down his wine glass. "I would be a hypocrite if I thought so, since your mother was only seventeen when we married." He sighed, then looked Ben in the eyes again. "I suppose I have no reason to ask you to wait so long. Will you at least allow enough time to call the banns? I see no need to procure a license from the bishop."

The anxiety that had weighed Ben down lifted, leaving him feeling light enough to float away. "I can promise that," he assured his father. "Lady Wilhelmina's family prefers the wedding to take place in Lancashire. It will take time to arrange everything."

Though her family had moved around a bit after her father's death, Willa said she still considered Selwyn Castle her home. It should be easy enough to arrange for the banns to be called both there and in Ben's home parish at Walbourne.

"I suppose that makes sense." Sir Lewis did not look precisely happy, but some of the concern had left his face. "Now that we have settled that, when will I get a chance to meet your intended?"

Ben leaned forward and began to happily plan that important introduction. With his father's approval, nothing stood in the way of the marriage.

Chapter Twenty

"WHAT DO YOU mean, Mr. Radcliffe is not accepting callers? He is expecting me this afternoon." Willa lifted her chin, hoping she looked confident rather than confused.

She did not normally stoop to arguing with servants. If a butler claimed an acquaintance was not at home, she accepted the social lie. But she could not imagine Ben turning her way. Could he have somehow forgotten their meeting?

"I am very sorry, my lady." Graves's limpid brown eyes looked genuinely regretful. "Mr. Radcliffe was taken ill late last night."

Willa put a hand to her mouth, but she was not quick enough to hide a gasp of dismay.

"I do not believe he is gravely ill, ma'am," Graves assured her. "His current indisposition appears similar to the digestive ailment he experienced some weeks ago."

"Oh." Willa frowned. "May not I visit the sick room? Only to take a peek at him?"

The somber look on Graves's face gave away the answer even before he shook his head. "I am afraid not, my lady. At the moment, he is too unwell to receive visitors. However, I will inform him of your call."

Willa walked back to town, trying to keep her disappointment from ruining the rest of the day. She had seen her fiancé only two days ago. It would not harm her to go another day without him.

She *had* looked forward to reading with him again, though. She was not convinced that Ben's "training" regimen would really lessen her aversion to the ocean, but she enjoyed sitting outside in pleasant weather, listening to his clear, sweet reading voice. She hated wasting such a clement day in early June. Who knew when they would again see such clear skies?

Willa fully expected to hear good news when next she called at Marlowe Tower. But the next day, the entire village buzzed with rumors about the ill-health at the Tower. Mr. Marlowe had fallen ill, too. Some people said he was at death's door. Others said no, it was his grandson who'd been most afflicted.

Finding it impossible to maintain her optimism in the face of these rumors, Willa dashed off a note to Miss Marlowe, asking if there was any way she might help. She hoped to receive a reassuring message in return.

Instead, Sir Lewis Radcliffe paid an unexpected morning call. He was as tall as Ben, but built more broadly, and he seemed to take up an inordinate amount of space in Cousin Sarah's little sitting room.

His presence there unsettled Willa. He was almost a stranger, but he would someday be her father-in-law. She had absolutely no idea how to speak to him.

Fortunately, Sir Lewis was at no loss for words. "I wish I were the bearer of better news, my dear, but Benjamin is very, very sick. I have sent to London for a better physician, as I am not satisfied with the medical man my father-in-law employs."

"No doubt there are physicians in London with far more learning," Willa agreed. "His illness is very serious, then?" She cast a nervous glance toward her mother, whose look of dismay probably mirrored her own.

"If you mean, is Benjamin in grave danger, no." Sir Lewis spoke slowly, apparently choosing his words with care. "But I do not like the fact that this is his second attack of severe dyspepsia.

Nor do I like the way the attacks seem to worsen."

Willa gulped. She had not thought of that. It *did* seem ominous. Did that mean Ben might get even more sick in the future?

Mama put a hand to her mouth. "Do you think it is something constitutional?" she whispered. "I have known people who suffer from life-long dyspepsia. It can make for a rather miserable life."

"Indeed." Sir Lewis sounded grim. "I certainly hope we are not dealing with anything like that." He studied Willa for a moment. "Though, if that is the case, it would be better for you to find out now, Lady Wilhelmina."

Willa wrinkled her forehead. Surely, he didn't mean that she should break the engagement on account of Ben's illness? What happened to "in sickness and in health"? She glanced towards her mother to gauge her reaction. To her surprise, her mother nodded in agreement.

"He is right, Wilhelmina. You would not wish to find yourself married to a perpetual invalid." Mama smiled reassuringly. "But I am sure Mr. Radcliffe has no such problems, especially since he is not the only one in the family who has fallen ill. There must be some other cause for the illnesses."

Such as what? It did not seem likely that tainted food was the problem since the gastric attacks had occurred several weeks apart. She could only hope that the London physician, when he arrived, would have a better theory.

WHEN BEN WAS finally declared well enough for visitors, Willa called on him, bringing a book about the Sandwich Islands and a letter from her mother's solicitor, outlining the progress that had been made on the settlements. Mr. Pritchard believed everything would be neatly tied up in time for a wedding at the beginning of July.

She found Ben sitting up in bed, a Paper Mache writing desk on his lap.

He eschewed traditional greetings in favor of exclaiming, "Willa! You're never going to believe what Dr. Gladwell thinks is making me sick."

"Does he blame your illness on food gone off?" Someone had placed a padded armchair beside the bed. Willa sat down, giving her skirt a surreptitious twitch to make it settle properly.

Ben's face fell. "How did you guess?"

Willa shrugged. "Since you are not the only one experiencing the digestive upsets, it can't be something constitutionally wrong with you." Thank goodness for that! "And if it were a contagious disease like cholera, wouldn't people outside of your household be getting sick, too?"

"That is exactly what he said." Ben's face brightened. "Did you know that you could think like a physician? I doubt most women can do that."

Willa raised her eyebrows. Did he realize what he had just implied? "I am merely thinking logically! Despite the nonsense people utter about the 'weaker sex,' women are just as logical as men. And just as illogical, too, sometimes," she admitted. "I don't think my mind is all that different from any other woman's."

Ben looked unconvinced. "I suppose you would know better than I how women think. I am sorry if I offended you. I merely meant to compliment you on your reasoning."

"It is not a compliment if it implies that others of my sex are in some way inferior. I do not think men and women differ much when it comes to powers of the mind. 'Excellence is pretty fairly divided between the sexes,'" she quoted.

He frowned. "I don't recognize that. What is it from?"

"*Northanger Abbey*. Henry Tilney says that to Catherine when they talk about whether women write better letters than men." She had always liked Henry's answer much more than the false chivalry that praised women for supposedly feminine skills while denying their abilities in more important matters.

"Women are sometimes better at replying to letters than men are," Ben pointed out. "But I suppose that is because they are encouraged to keep up a voluminous personal correspondence."

"Precisely. I believe many of the differences between women and men come down to education and upbringing rather than nature." What a comfort it was to be able to say things like that to Ben! In Willa's experience, many gentlemen disliked having their supposed superiority challenged. But Ben's thoughtful expression did not change.

"You may be right," he granted. "It would be a difficult subject to investigate scientifically, though. Unless one decided to rear one's sons and daughters identically and then see whether any of the supposedly natural differences still existed—"

Willa interrupted before he could become too invested in that idea. "I am not sure it is appropriate to use one's children in a scientific experiment."

"I suppose not." A crooked smile slanted across his face. "But it would be even worse to experiment with someone else's children, wouldn't it?"

She put a hand to her mouth to conceal her own smile. "Very true," she agreed. "But setting aside the morality of performing experiments on children, does the new doctor have any suggestions about how to *avoid* this illness?" At the moment, that seemed a far more pressing concern.

Ben grimaced. "Dr. Gladwell suggested that Grandfather fire Mrs. Kirby. She's our cook," he added, though Willa had guessed as much. "But she has worked here for over ten years, so it doesn't make sense to blame her for the recent illnesses. If she were doing something wrong, people ought to have been sick before now."

Willa nodded. She understood why Dr. Gladwell might blame the cook, but unless there were recent changes in how Mrs. Kirby managed the kitchen, that theory made little sense.

Ben leaned forward, resting his elbows on the writing desk. "*My* guess is that someone is selling adulterated food or drink."

She blinked. "Adulterated? How so?"

"Have you heard about the way people sometimes water down milk, then add chalk to make it look white?"

Willa wrinkled her nose. "Chalk? Ugh! Could that be what made you so sick?

He shook his head. "No, Dr. Gladwell says chalk would not irritate one's digestive system that much. Believe me, I asked about it—not that I think our dairyman would do such a thing."

"Oh, right. You probably get your milk from your own farm." Probably most people who could afford to keep their own dairy cattle did. Willa had always assumed that keeping dairy cows was a matter of convenience and economy. It had never occurred to her that there might be health risks involved in buying milk from someone you could not trust.

But people in cities could not keep cattle. What, she wondered, happened to children who grew up drinking adulterated milk?

"Yes, precisely. But there are other substances more harmful than chalk that can be mixed into food. Dr. Gladwell mentioned that there have been tragic poisonings when someone mistook rat poison or weed killer for a cooking ingredient."

Willa shuddered at the prospect of eating rat poison, but for some reason, Ben's face brightened. "Dr. Gladwell was not able to answer all of my questions about common poisons, so I sent off to London for a treatise on toxicology," he confided. "I hope it gets here next week."

She pursed her lips, wondering why the possibility of poison excited him so much. Then she remembered that he liked complicated problems. He'd told her as much, weeks ago. It was why he'd first become interested in her phobia.

Ben might view this illness as an intellectual challenge, but to Willa, it was a real threat. What if the next attack proved fatal—if not to Ben, then to his aunt or grandfather? It had taken his aunt weeks to recover after her illness. So far as she knew, Mr. Marlowe was still very ill.

"Does Dr. Gladwell have any guesses about what substance could be making everyone sick?" she wondered.

Some of the light faded from Ben's eyes. "He listed a few possibilities, but he says that without a sample of the contaminated food, there's no way to determine what pollutant is involved."

"He could take samples of all the food in the kitchen. . . I suppose that isn't practical, is it?" Willa frowned as she thought about the problem. "Is there any way to narrow down which foods are most likely to have been tainted?"

"That is what I was working on before you showed up!" Ben handed her a sheet of paper with neatly labelled columns. "I am trying to list everything we ate the day before I fell sick. I will need Aunt Faith's help, though, because I do not know what she and Grandfather ate."

Indeed, the only one of the columns that had been filled out was the one under Ben's own name. Willa's mouth watered as she read over the list: rolls, butter, and tea with milk for breakfast; cold meat, bread, and cucumber salad at luncheon. The extensive dinner menu included fresh fish, a casseroled chicken, spring lamb with spring peas, and duckling with carrots and spring potatoes. The meal had been accompanied by both red wine and white wine and followed by port, cheese, and biscuits.

By the time she finished the list, Willa's stomach was starting to rumble. She had to forcibly remind herself that something on this list had made Ben very, very sick. Apart from that, it all sounded quite appealing.

"Did your grandfather eat most of the same foods?" she wondered.

Ben shook his head. "He did not eat the lamb, because it was too fatty, nor the fish, because he was afraid it might not be fresh enough. I do not remember whether he ate all the other foods. But the servants would have finished off whatever we did not eat, so it is surprising that none of them are ill."

She handed him back the list. "This is going to be an enormous task, isn't it?" She felt tired merely thinking about all the people Ben would have to interrogate in order to figure out who ate what. And of course, most people wouldn't remember what they ate after so much time had passed.

"Yes." The lines in his forehead deepened as he looked over the list. "Even I cannot be sure whether I tasted everything on the menu. I usually dislike food cooked *à la casserole*, but I had to leave that dish on the list because I could not remember if I tasted it."

"What do you have against chicken *à la casserole?*" Willa thought it sounded delicious, but maybe that was only because she was hungry.

He shuddered. "I do not like foods that mix different textures. Except pies, I suppose. I like meat pies. But foods that have a layer of this and a layer of that, or that mix soft foods with firmer ones—they often bother me." He pulled a rueful smile. "I know that probably sounds strange, but I have always been that way. Some foods simply do not feel good in my mouth."

"Interesting." She probably ought to write these kinds of preferences down, Willa thought absently. No point in having their future cook prepare food *à la casserole* if Ben never ate it! "And you ate nothing after dinner? No tea or coffee?"

"Hmm? No, I don't think—oh, I had a cup of chocolate just before bed! Thank you for reminding me." He scrawled that at the bottom of the list. "I remember asking Mrs. Kirby to use extra sugar. I was in the mood for something sweet that night."

"Chocolate *seems* innocent enough," Willa mused. "But it uses milk and sugar and spices. Any of those could have been adulterated." She gnawed on her lip, and her stomach gurgled again. "I don't suppose there are any biscuits in the kitchen?" she asked hopefully.

"Don't eat anything here!"

Her jaw dropped. She had never heard Ben speak so sharply. "What on earth. . .?"

Ben ran a hand through his already-unruly hair. "Sorry. I did not mean to snap. But since we have no idea what might be making us sick, you should not eat anything from our kitchen. Just to be safe."

Willa felt touched by his concern, though she hoped it was unnecessary. "I suppose you are right to worry." Then a new idea struck her. "If I *did* get sick, that would help you figure out which food was contaminated, wouldn't it? Maybe—"

"Absolutely not." Perhaps he didn't quite glare at her, but he came closer to glaring than she'd ever seen. "You must not experiment on yourself."

She pretended to pout for a moment before giving in. "Very well. But that might mean I have to go home for my tea."

"My aunt will probably kick you out of my room soon any-way," he warned. "She thinks I am too ill for long visits. But will you come back to see me tomorrow?"

"Of course!" She leaned forward to brush a kiss against his cheek before she left.

On the way home, it occurred to her that though Ben was concerned for *her* safety, he might be tempted to experiment on himself. Next time she saw him, she must make him promise not to do so. He was by no means expendable.

Chapter Twenty-One

THIS TIME, BEN'S stomach took longer to heal than after the previous bouts of sickness. He wondered if the mystery food that had sickened him might be somehow accumulating in this body. All he knew for certain, though, was that his stomach hurt after every meal. The pins-and-needles sensation in his fingers and toes lingered, too.

On account of his irritated digestive system, Ben faithfully followed the doctor's advice and restricted himself to beef tea and toast. It wasn't particularly difficult, given how little desire for food he felt. Even the hours he spent writing notes about past meals did little to stimulate his appetite.

Unfortunately, the notes did nothing to stimulate his powers of problem-solving, either. He'd done his best to recall what he had eaten each of the times he'd been sick. The housekeeper's menu book was an enormous help, as it listed what had been served at every dinner and luncheon. But neither the housekeeper nor the cook recorded which members of the household had eaten specific foods, leaving Ben to rely on faulty human memory.

Still, between the menu book, his memory, and conversations with Mrs. Kirby, he had a good idea of what foods could have been involved in the earlier gastric attacks. The problem was that he could see no pattern.

There were some foods and beverages that he consumed nearly every day: sweet rolls and tea at breakfast; port wine and biscuits at night. But why would those foods make him sick one day and not another? Or why would the tainted food sicken one member of the family one time, but not the others?

There must be some explanation, but he could not figure it out. Which meant he had no idea what to do to prevent another attack. Ben might be healthy enough to bounce back from such an illness, but the same could not be said for his grandfather and his aunt.

He was still looking over his notes when he heard footsteps pounding down the hall. He stacked all the loose pieces of foolscap together, slipped out of bed, and hurried to see what was going on.

When he realized the hubbub centered on the master suite, Ben had an unpleasant hunch about what happened. His grandfather's condition must have taken a sudden turn for the worse.

Indeed, when Ben peered into the room, he saw his grandfather doubled over, retching into a basin. One of the footmen supported him, while Aunt Faith hovered anxiously nearby, holding a washcloth. She caught Ben's eye and subtly shook her head. Evidently, she didn't want him to witness this.

Ben retreated to his room, mind teeming with eager questions. What would have caused Grandfather Marlowe's relapse? Why was he vomiting again, when Ben was not? *What had he eaten today?*

He did not get a chance to ask those questions until much later in the day. Dr. Gladwell had long since returned to London, so Dr. Milner was summoned to his bedside. After examining Grandfather Marlowe, the physician held a hushed consultation with Ben's father and aunt.

Despite his protests, Ben was excluded from this meeting. Unwilling to give up his quest for information, he hovered in the entryway, biding his time. When Dr. Milner headed for the doorway, Ben pounced.

Dr. Milner was so startled he literally flinched like a shying horse. "Ah, Mr. Radcliffe! Good to see that you are doing so well today."

"How is my grandfather doing? Do you know why he relapsed?"

The physician sighed and lowered the hat he'd been about to don. "Your aunt can probably explain the situation about as well as I can," he grumbled. "I do not know why he relapsed. I would think it was something he ate, but he has had nothing but tea and toast today. I suppose it could have been the milk in the tea, since some people react poorly to milk, but who knows?" He raised his hands in a "what can you do?" gesture.

Ben frowned. "Hmm. I don't think it could be the milk, since I added milk to my tea, too. I don't feel at all unwell today."

"As did your aunt," Dr. Milner said. "I must confess, I am out of ideas. We can only treat Mr. Marlowe's symptoms and hope for the best. Now, if you'll excuse me?"

Ben stepped aside, hardly noticing when the door shut behind the doctor. By then, he was already deep in thought. He paced back and forth in the entryway, trying to work through all the possibilities.

Thus, when someone knocked a few minutes later, Ben opened the door before either of the footmen could reach it. "Oh, Willa! It's good that you're here. There's a new wrinkle in the case."

She blinked at him, apparently startled by this untraditional greeting. "Oh? What now?"

He led her upstairs, while catching her up to speed on the newest developments. "So you see, this complicates our theory about food contamination." He sat down on the edge of his bed and handed her the stack of papers. "I've spent hours poring over all the details I could find about everyone's diet before each attack of gastritis, but I haven't discovered any pattern. And I am usually good at detecting patterns!"

"Hmm." She sat down and began flipping through the stack of papers. "What did your grandfather eat today? Or yesterday?"

He shuffled through the pages until he found the one with today's breakfast. "The same thing I ate and drank—merely black tea and buttered toast." He tapped the relevant lines. "My aunt insisted we weren't well enough for anything stronger yet. You see, that's what doesn't make sense to me. If Grandfather and I ate the same things, why did he take a turn for the worse when I did not?"

"Does he take his tea the same way?" she asked. "Did you both put butter on the toast?"

He shook his head because he'd already thought of that. "It can't be the butter or the milk, because I take my tea with milk, too."

"Milk and no sugar?" she asked. "Is that how you both take it?"

Ben stilled. "Grandfather takes his tea with sugar, but I do not." He stared down at the paper. He hadn't written "sugar" on the page. He probably hadn't recorded it for any of the meals.

"That's right. You told me you took sugar in your chocolate, but not tea and coffee." Willa wrinkled her forehead as she thought. "Did you have anything sweetened with sugar before your illness?"

Ben sat still as he ransacked his memory. "Now that you mention it, I had a cup of chocolate the night before my latest attack." His heart began to beat more quickly. "It had sugar in it." A look laden with meaning passed between them.

"But how would something toxic have gotten in the sugar?" Willa wondered.

"We may be jumping ahead too quickly," Ben warned. They did not even know for certain that Grandfather Marlowe had taken sugar with his tea today. His illness could have thrown him off his usual tastes. "I will have to ask—"

The door to Ben's room abruptly swung open, startling them both.

"Ben? Who are you—oh! Lady Wilhelmina! I did not realize you were here." His father stood in the doorway, momentarily dumbfounded. Gradually, his look of surprise turned into disapproval. "Benjamin, if you wish to entertain guests, the morning room is free. But you must not tire yourself out with visitors. We do not want you to have a relapse, too."

Ben opened his mouth, intending to remind his father that Grandfather Marlowe had experienced a relapse without receiving a single visitor today or yesterday. The stern expression on his father's face changed his mind. "Yes, we should go down to the morning room."

"I can only stay for a few minutes, anyway," Willa chimed in. "I have, ah, errands to do."

The corner of Ben's mouth kicked up in a smile. He was fairly certain that Willa had invented those "errands" at a moment's notice.

He escorted Willa back downstairs, still thinking about the sugar theory. "I need to find out whether my grandfather took sugar in his tea today or yesterday. I should probably ask Mrs. Kirby some questions about the source of the sugar, too."

"I wish I could stay and help you investigate, but I really ought to go back home." Willa tipped her head back to look him in the eyes as she whispered, "I don't think your father was happy to see me here today."

Ben had to agree. "He was unhappy because you were in my bedroom," he reminded her. "He probably thought we were up to no good." Being betrothed might make it easier to spend time with Willa, but there were still rules. Apparently, Ben had broken them without realizing it.

Willa softly chuckled. "Little does he know that you are too preoccupied with toxins to plan a seduction right now."

"Yes, quite," he murmured, only half paying attention. He was distracted by the question of when he had eaten or drunk something sweetened with sugar.

If the sugar were toxic, wouldn't all of Mrs. Kirby's desserts have made people ill? But Ben had consumed biscuits, cakes, and puddings from her kitchen without ill effects. So had Aunt Faith and Willa and a handful of other guests who'd dined at Marlowe Tower over the last few months.

Willa sighed. "Well, good-bye then." She stood on her toes to press a kiss against his cheek. He waved a silent farewell and returned to his pacing.

Only after she left did it occur to Ben that she might have been unhappy about his preoccupation with the case. Had she *wanted* him to seduce her? Surely not!

BEN HAD TO time his visit to the kitchen carefully. He knew better than to interrupt in the middle of dinner preparation. Fortunately, he caught Mrs. Kirby just before she began preparing a chicken for roasting.

"It's funny you should ask about the sugar," Mrs. Kirby said. "We had a full cannister of it that vanished into thin air. We had to buy more!" She leaned against the heavy kitchen table. "We were lucky the sugar bowl was still full."

"The sugar bowl for the tea set, you mean?" Ben asked.

"Yes, full to the brim it was," one of the kitchen maids chimed in. "When you asked for chocolate the other day, I took the sugar from that bowl, because we couldn't find our main supply."

A thrill coursed through Ben. The chocolate he drank the night he fell sick had been sweetened from the same source that sweetened Grandfather's tea. *This was it.* He was certain of it.

"What about the sugar in the bowl now?" he asked eagerly. "Is it the same as what you put in the chocolate?"

"That I do not know," the cook admitted. "Carrie?" She looked towards the maid.

"I don't believe the sugar bowl has been refilled yet," the

maid said. "Mr. Marlowe is the only one who normally takes sugar in his tea, and with him so sick, there hasn't been much call for it. I think there's a little left."

"Can I see it?" Ben asked hopefully. Then he modified the request. "Actually, can I take what is left in the bowl, in order to examine it? I have some, um, experiments to do with it."

The maid and the cook exchanged puzzled looks. Then Mrs. Kirby shrugged. "I don't see what that would hurt. We've more sugar in the pantry now. But what kind of experiment is it?"

"An experiment in toxicology."

Mrs. Kirby looked none the wiser for his explanation, but she asked no more questions. She refused to let Ben take the bowl itself, so he poured its contents into an empty stoneware crock and carried it off to the carriage house. He knew without even asking that his aunt would not want him conducting chemical experiments in the house.

Not that he knew what kind of experiment he needed to conduct. He had read a little about chemistry now and then, but there were large gaps in his knowledge. He had certainly never studied poison.

Fortunately, he knew where to look for directions, because his copy of Orfila's *General System of Toxicology* had finally arrived from London. Today, he'd sit down with the book and dig in. Orfila was the most significant living scholar writing about toxicology. Ben was confident that he would find the answers there.

Chapter Twenty-Two

W HEN WILLA CALLED the next day, Graves directed her to the carriage house. By now, she knew the way to Ben's workroom, so she declined the offer of an escort.

She found her fiancé sitting at the table in the center of the room. He looked in reasonably good health, except that losing weight had left his face a bit gaunt.

"Good afternoon!" Willa called.

He flinched like a startled horse but relaxed when he looked up and saw who it was. "Arsenic!" he exclaimed, apropos of nothing.

"Arsenic to you, too!" she replied.

Ben cocked his head, looking baffled.

"'Arsenic' is an interesting salutation." Willa hung her bonnet on a peg by the door. "In what country do people greet each other that way?"

"Oh, you are joking." Ben shook his head. "For a moment I thought I needed to explain what arsenic was."

"I do know that much." Arsenic was such a common poison that nearly everyone would have heard of it. "I read a book about the Italian Renaissance that discussed arsenic. At one time, arsenic was a popular poison in Italy. People used it to dispose of their political enemies." She took the chair next to Ben. "I suppose we should have thought of it earlier. Arsenic is supposed to be tasteless, isn't it?"

"Precisely," he agreed. "Oxide of arsenic dissolves in water and has neither taste nor smell. More importantly, it looks much like sugar." He took the lid off a small stoneware crock and tipped it toward her so she could see the contents.

Willa's eyes widened. "Is that arsenic?" she breathed.

"I do not know yet," he admitted. "Some of it is sugar. I can tell that much from the taste."

Willa gasped. "You tasted poison?" Why on earth would he risk getting sick again? Hadn't he had enough stomach trouble to last a lifetime?

"I only put a little bit of it at the tip of my tongue," he explained. "Just enough to tell that it was sweet, which means some of this is sugar. But I suspect arsenic has been mixed in."

"How can we tell for certain?"

"Well," he said slowly, "There are experiments you can do to identify arsenic, but I don't know how the addition of sugar might affect the experiment. If I put this over a fire, the sugar would burn, wouldn't it? And I do not know enough about chemistry to know if that would affect the chemical tests for arsenic."

"You need to consult a chemist, then," Willa suggested.

He nodded. "Fortunately, Dr. Gladwell has already been summoned to attend Grandfather. I am sure he will know what to do with this." He put the lid back on the crock of poison. "In the meantime, we should think about how the arsenic could have gotten mixed in with the sugar."

"Ah. You know, I have been thinking about that question since yesterday."

"Yes?" Eager interest filled his face.

Willa hesitated, trying to get the words in the best order. "The only reason I knew who took sugar in their tea was because your cousin Almeria asked about it the night I dined with the Millingtons. Do you remember that?"

"Oh, yes. How *did* that subject come up in conversation, anyway? It seems an odd subject."

"Yes, very odd," Willa said firmly. "It came up out of nowhere, and I remember wondering at the time why Miss Millington should care whether you or your aunt took your tea with sugar. She explicitly asked if your grandfather was the only one who used sugar."

She drew a deep breath before asking what she suspected was a crucial question. "Ben, who inherits your grandfather's estate when he passes away? Will it go to your aunt?" She held her breath as she studied his reaction.

Ben scratched his head. "I believe the will stipulates that Aunt Faith has the right to live here rent-free all her life, but my grandfather has always said that the ownership of the house will pass to a family with children. I assume the Millington family would inherit it, because they need it more than my family does."

That was what Willa would have guessed, too. Ben was already heir to his father's baronetcy. According to her family's solicitor, the Radcliffe estate was thriving. Ben did not need a second estate or an additional fortune.

"Would either Marlowe or Almeria be desperate enough for that fortune that they might kill to get it sooner rather than later?" She whispered the question, though there was no chance of their being overheard. Then she bit her lip, half-afraid Ben would lose his temper at that accusation.

But he remained as calm as ever, apart from drumming his fingers on the table as he pondered the question. "I would not have thought it of either of them, but I cannot rule it out. The Millingtons probably stand to gain the most if Grandfather dies." His frown deepened as he asked, "But why would they want to kill *me?*"

"A good question," Willa admitted. The only reason for the Millingtons to kill Ben would be if they thought he stood in the way of their inheritance. But there was no reason to think that. "Could your illnesses have been accidental? Perhaps you weren't intended to consume the poison."

"But that makes no sense either!" he protested. "I had my first case of gastritis weeks before my grandfather did, and Aunt Faith nearly died after the picnic. If Grandfather Marlowe was the target all along, our poisoner must be remarkably inept."

The picnic! Willa gnawed on her lower as she teased out an idea. "Ben, didn't your cousin Almeria make that fruitcake you brought to the picnic? The one that reeked of rum?"

His eyes widened. "Yes. Good heavens, you are right. Why didn't I remember that?"

Willa grinned. "Probably because fruitcake did not seem important. You didn't eat any of it, did you?" He shook his head. "Neither did I. I think Cousin Sarah tried a little bit, but the only person who ate more than a slice was—"

He finished the sentence for her. "My aunt. Aunt Faith was the only one at the picnic who really liked the fruitcake. I think she had a couple of slices." He stared off into the distance for a moment, then flicked his gaze back to her. "You must be right. Almeria must have poisoned the fruitcake. She would have thought Grandfather would eat it—he used to love that recipe. She might not have intended Aunt Faith to get sick at all."

A delicious thrill of excitement swept through Willa. She loved being the one who got the right answer. "It all fits, doesn't it?"

But Ben frowned again. "The fruitcake and the sugar explain the two most recent poisonings, but what made me sick at the end of April?"

"Were there any other foods your cousins sent?" Willa suggested. She and Ben would not be able to prove the identity of the poisoner unless they could propose a possible vehicle for the poison.

"I don't think so. Marlowe didn't bring any food with him when he visited, so far as I remember. In fact. . ." His voice trailed off.

Then, to her surprise, Ben got up from his chair and walked over to one of the shelves. He lifted up a fat blue crock. Then he turned to Willa. "Do you remember that jar full of peppermints I had in here the first time you visited?"

"I think so," Willa said. "But it was a different jar, wasn't it? I remember a glass jar."

He nodded and put the little crock back on the shelf. "Yes. That jar broke when Marlowe knocked it off the table. There was glass everywhere, and I had to throw out all the peppermints."

It took Willa a moment to make the connection. "You think the peppermints were poisoned, and Marlowe spilled them on purpose to prevent your eating them?" Doubt filled her voice. It seemed like a bit of a stretch to her.

"Remember, I'm not the one who likes peppermints. The peppermints were supposed to be for my grandfather, too. Everyone in the family knows he loved them. He avoids sweets now because they hurt his teeth, but Almeria and Marlowe probably didn't know that."

"Just as they didn't know that fruitcake is too rich for his digestion now." The more she thought about it, the more possible it seemed. "If that's right, then all the poisonings were accidents, except for when your grandfather got sick." The Millingtons did not seem like very efficient poisoners.

"He is still very ill. The Millingtons may succeed in murdering him yet." Ben sounded grim, and no wonder, if his cousins were trying to kill his grandfather!

"But if we know what is poisoning him, the doctor might know how to treat it," she pointed out. If arsenic poisoning *could* be treated. She knew there were some poisons that had no antidote.

"I certainly hope so. Maybe Orfila has some suggestions." Ben reached for a heavy leather-bound volume that rested on the table. "This is the treatise on toxicology I consulted, It helped me identify the arsenic, but it might also—"

"Ben?"

An ominous sense of familiarity struck Willa as she turned toward the doorway. Ben's father glowered there, hands resting on his hips. The panicked look on Ben's face was quickly followed by shame. He hung his head, and the tops of his ears burned red.

"Benjamin, when last we spoke on the subject of propriety, I thought you understood what was at stake." Sir Lewis did not raise his voice, but his anger was palpable despite the softness of his voice. "I am very sorry to discover otherwise."

Willa jumped into the fray, hoping to help. "Sir, it was not Ben's fault. I should have asked for a maid to accompany me here. Ben is no more guilty of impropriety than am I." She ought to have remembered that even betrothed couples were not generally left alone behind closed doors—at least not for long periods of time.

"That may be, my lady," Sir Lewis said gently, "but it is Ben's responsibility to treat you with all the respect due to your rank, age, and situation in life. Until your wedding, your reputation must be protected."

"Yes, sir." Ben rose to his feet. "Willa and I can return to the house—"

"No," Sir Lewis interrupted. "I will accompany Lady Wilhelmina home. I wish to speak with her."

Willa and Ben exchanged uneasy glances. *I am not a child,* Willa reminded herself. And even if she had still been a schoolgirl, Sir Lewis had no right to scold her! He was neither her parent nor her guardian.

She walked out of the room with her chin held high, hoping to disguise the sweatiness of her hands and the rapid beating of her heart. But she doubted she fooled Sir Lewis once he offered her his arm for support. Her nervousness must have been palpable.

"You need not be afraid, my dear. I have no desire to act the part of an overbearing father with you." The faint emphasis on "you" suggested Ben might not be so lucky. "I am, however, concerned that my son is not demonstrating the maturity required of a young man who intends to be set up his own household."

It took Willa a moment to parse that. "Do you mean to say

that because he sometimes forgets about propriety, he is not ready for matrimony?" If so, that surprised her. Most people thought a young man who kept running into scandal would do better in wedlock, as if having a wife would prevent future indiscretions.

"You may have perhaps noticed that Benjamin can be absent-minded," Sir Lewis said drily.

The corners of Willa's mouth quirked up. It would be hard for anyone who knew Ben not to notice that! "There is nothing wrong with his mind," Willa explained. "When he focuses on one subject, he may forget about others, but that could happen to anyone." How often had Cousin Sarah left the house, only to hurry back when she discovered she had left behind her reticule, her umbrella, or something of equal importance?

The baronet looked down at her and smiled wryly. "But you cannot deny that it happens more often to Ben than to most people."

She hung her head, knowing he was right. "I am not sure Ben can prevent that, though. That may just be part of who he is."

The corners of Sir Lewis's mouth tipped down. "I do not think it is unreasonable to expect Ben to remember that people will gossip about the two of you if you keep meeting alone, behind closed doors. And the gossip will hurt you far more than it does him, my lady. If he cannot behave responsibly in so simple a case as this, what will he do when more challenging situations arise?"

His frown looked thoughtful rather than angry as he added, "And challenges *will* arise, you know. Everyone encounters troubles of one sort or another. Married life may be a joy, but it is not a fairy tale."

Willa flushed. "I have never thought it was a fairy tale!" Hearing the angry bite in her voice, she paused to collect herself before continuing. "All I say is that Ben is preoccupied with important concerns at the moment."

"More important than your reputation?" He lifted his brows.

"Yes," she said firmly. Murder was certainly more important than scandal. "I think you should talk to him about what he has discovered. It might well be a matter of life and death."

Sir Lewis's mouth gaped open, though he recovered quickly. "Well, I certainly shall speak to Ben. But in the meantime, I would prefer you to refrain from disturbing his healing process."

Willa tipped her head back to peer up at him. He looked serious. "You mean, I am not to visit anymore?" she guessed.

"Not at the moment. I believe Benjamin has some hard thinking to do." They parted on that cryptic note, leaving Willa full of questions.

✦

Chapter Twenty-Three

B EN MORE OR less expected his relatives to greet his arsenic theory with disbelief. Though Marlowe Millington had caused trouble throughout his boyhood, Almeria had always been a pattern of perfection. Poisoning her grandfather for personal gain seemed out of character, to say the very least.

However, Ben was not prepared for his father to lay down an ultimatum after Ben discussed his poisoning theory.

"You need to think about where your priorities are, young man." Sir Lewis sat in the study, behind Grandfather Marlowe's desk, his hands neatly folded on the desktop. Between his scowl and his ramrod-straight posture, he gave the impression of a stern headmaster scolding a problem pupil.

His father's attitude set Ben's teeth on edge. He counted down from three, trying to calm himself enough to answer Sir Lewis.

But Sir Lewis spoke before Ben could formulate a reply. "I understand that you prefer the life of the mind over most social functions, Benjamin. And for the most part, your mother and I accept that. But even the most abstract thinker must sometimes deal with the practicalities of day-to-day life."

"I do not understand what this has to do with the cause of my recurring stomach upsets," Ben interjected. "Why are you changing the subject?" He had not yet explained all the evidence that supported his arsenic theory.

His father sighed and rubbed his forehead. "I am changing the subject because I think you need to take a close look at yourself and decide what is most important to you. Do you want to continue being an oblivious bookworm, or are you ready to embrace the responsibilities that come with adulthood?"

"What on earth do you mean?" Ben stared blankly. He still did not understand where his father was going with this argument, but he suspected he wasn't going to like the destination.

"As I see it, you can continue to build castles-in-the-air about poison and murder, or you can focus on preparing yourself for managing a household and family." His father caught Ben's gaze and refused to let him look away. "If you continue to prioritize this ridiculous investigation over your very real responsibilities, I will no longer support your betrothal."

Ben's jaw dropped. For a long, painful moment, the only sound he heard was the beating of his own heart. How could that organ continue its steady, patient rhythm, when the rug had just been yanked out from under his feet?

"You can't stop me from marrying someone," he reminded his father. "I am not a minor." Only people under the age of twenty-one needed parental approval to marry.

"Very true," his father agreed. "But I can withdraw the financial support promised in the settlements. Do you think Lady Wilhelmina's family will allow her to marry you without that income? You may not be a minor, but she *is*."

Feeling numb, Ben could only shake his head in dismay. His father was probably right. The Selwyn family had approved Willa's betrothal because Sir Lewis had formally agreed to provide the couple with a modest home and an allowance. Willa's family would probably not agree to her marrying a penniless man.

Ben stood to inherit a comfortable estate, but his father was still relatively young and in good health. Sir Lewis might yet live for decades. Ben did not, could not, expect Willa to wait decades to marry him. Their engagement would undoubtedly end if Sir Lewis withdrew his support.

"So, you are giving me an ultimatum, is that it? Either I give up investigating a suspected crime, or I abandon my intended bride." He shook his head again. Sir Lewis had never truly understood Ben, but it was not like him to be so hard!

"Yes, that is about the long and short of it," Sir Lewis agreed. "Now, if you'll excuse me, I have some letters to write."

Ben rose from his chair and stumbled away, stunned by the threat. It made no sense to him. If Sir Lewis was genuinely concerned about Ben's well-being, shouldn't he be glad that Ben had found some possible answers to all their questions about these strange digestive attacks?

In times of trouble, Ben liked to surround himself with familiar things. So, still walking in a daze, he made his way back to his workroom. He sat down at the table and stared at the toxicology book that had first put him on the right path.

If Ben were right, two of his cousins had tried to commit murder. A crime like that could not be ignored, especially since Grandfather Marlowe's life might still be in danger. Turning away from the investigation would be almost a crime of its own.

But a gentleman was never supposed to break a betrothal, either. That was the lady's prerogative. Only a scoundrel would jilt a woman after she accepted his proposal. True, it would not be breach of promise if Willa herself broke off the engagement due to lack of financial support. But it would still be ethically wrong, even if not legally wrong.

Ben's father had set him an impossible choice. How could he choose between doing the right thing and loving the right person?

BY THE TIME Dr. Gladwell arrived, Ben had made up his mind. He let the elder family members talk to the physician first. Then, when Dr. Gladwell examined Ben to confirm his recovery, Ben revealed his theory.

Dr. Gladwell turned out to be an ideal listener. He sat patiently while Ben listed all the reasons why he thought the gastric illness might have been caused by arsenic, along with the ways he thought the arsenic had been administered and the people who might have had motive and opportunity to commit the crime.

"Do you mean to say that you have a sample of the poison?" Dr. Gladwell asked.

Ever precise, Ben clarified, "I have a sample that I believe contains poison intermingled with sugar. I did not feel confident enough about my knowledge of chemistry to try testing it to see if it really is arsenic."

He studied the physician's face for a moment. Dr. Gladwell looked interested and thoughtful rather than dismissive. "Would you like to see the sample?" he offered.

"Yes, if you please. I am no chemist myself, but your local apothecary should have all the equipment needed to test for arsenic."

Ben dashed off to his workroom. As he ran down the corridor, he startled his aunt.

"What's the rush?" she asked.

"No time to explain," he called over his shoulder. "It's a medical problem." Which was perfectly true, even if it was not the full truth. If he were directly asked about this investigation, Ben would tell the truth, but he saw no need to volunteer more information than necessary.

Dr. Gladwell continued to wear that thoughtful frown as he examined the white crystals Ben had found in the sugar bowl. But he revealed nothing of what he thought.

"Well?" Ben prompted when he could no longer stand the suspense.

Dr. Gladwell replaced the lid on the container. "It is possible, young man. It is possible," he said judiciously. "More than that I cannot say. May I take this sample with me into town? I would like to consult someone with a better knowledge of chemistry."

"Yes, of course." It was on the tip of Ben's tongue to ask if he could tag along, but he decided against it. There was no point in unnecessarily angering his father. If Ben left the investigation in Dr. Gladwell's hands, he could honestly say that he had given it up.

When his aunt suggested that Ben should rest, he took to the couch with a novel in hand, pretending to recuperate. He might look the picture of innocence, but while his hands held the first volume of a G.W. Kirkland novel, his mind wandered through a labyrinth of possibilities. If the sugar really did contain arsenic, what would happen next? Would the local magistrate be summoned? And if the sugar did not contain arsenic, what *did* cause the epidemic at Marlowe Tower? Would they ever discover the truth?

Dressing for dinner did not put a stop to Ben's speculations. He continued thinking about the suspected poisoning even after he joined his aunt and his father in the drawing room. Aunt Faith, who looked exhausted, sat with a glass of sherry in hand. Sir Lewis paced back and forth.

"Any changes in Grandfather's condition?" Ben asked.

Aunt Faith merely sighed and shook her head. His father was the one who answered. "No improvements yet. He still complains of stomach pain, thirst, and cold, though he has no fever."

Symptoms of arsenic poisoning! Ben turned to pour himself a glass of sherry, not because he wanted a drink, but to hide his triumph. When would Dr. Gladwell return? He could not wait to learn if his theory was correct.

Graves opened the drawing room door, and everyone turned, assuming that dinner was ready. Instead, the butler announced, "Mr. Millington."

In his surprise, Ben actually spilled sherry onto the floor. "Marlowe, what are you doing here?" Had he come to finish the murder he'd started?

"Is that any way to greet your favorite cousin?" Marlowe

flung himself into an armchair, propping his feet up on a nearby footrest. "Am I late for dinner?"

"Just in time." Aunt Faith sounded wearier than ever. Ben suspected he wasn't the only one annoyed by Marlowe's unexpected arrival.

Even Graves looked frankly irritated as he said, "I will add another place setting to the table."

Throughout dinner, Ben alternated between anxiously wondering when he would learn the results of Dr. Gladwell's investigation and worrying about Marlowe's intentions. If Ben were right and the Millington cousins were trying to murder their grandfather, Marlowe ought to be supervised at all times to prevent further harm.

On the other hand, if Ben even so much as hinted at the possibility that Marlowe meant to harm anyone, Sir Lewis might carry out his threat to withdraw support for the betrothal. Moreover, Marlowe would undoubtedly be furious if Ben accused him of attempted murder. Such accusations could lead to permanent estrangements between relatives.

It was a relief when the meal ended, and an even bigger relief when Ben's father suggested that the gentlemen join Aunt Faith in the drawing room instead of lingering over their port. By that time, Ben had formulated a plan for dealing with Marlowe. He only hoped he'd have the chance to carry it out.

When Graves brought out the tea tray, Ben came to attention like a hunting dog that had just scented a covey. There sat the sugar bowl that Ben believed had once contained poison. It had since been thoroughly cleaned and filled with pure, refined sugar. . . but Marlowe wouldn't know that.

Ben maneuvered into place by Marlowe's side while Aunt Faith poured tea. While Marlowe watched, Ben dumped three spoonsful of sugar into his teacup and stirred vigorously. Aunt Faith, who knew very well that Ben did not take sugar, scrunched up her face in confusion.

"I have a craving for something sweet," Ben told her. Then he turned to his cousin. "I say, Marlowe, I like the way you tied your cravat tonight. What do you call it?"

Marlowe, who knew that Ben cared little about fashion, stared blankly at him. Then he glanced down at his cravat. "Er. . . it is just a barrel knot. Nothing terribly fancy."

"Tied it yourself, did you? Do you suppose you can show me how you do it?"

"Er, I suppose?" Though Marlowe still looked confused, he began to unwind his cravat. "I did not know you needed this much help with your neck cloth, Ben," he sneered.

While Marlowe was distracted, Ben put his own teacup down on the table a mere inch away from Marlowe's cup.

This was the trickiest part of Ben's plan, and he more than half expected it to fail. Incredibly, it worked: Marlowe was so busy looking down at his cravat that he did not notice when Ben switched the cups, moving the heavily sugared tea to where Marlowe's cup had rested a moment ago.

Ben lifted the teacup he'd swapped from Marlowe, as if he were about to drink, but he kept his eyes fixed on his cousin.

"Is something wrong?" Marlowe asked. "Am I tying this crookedly?" He squinted down at the cravat.

"No, no," Ben said. "I was merely distracted by a passing thought." Trying to look natural, he lowered his eyes and took a sip of what should have been Marlowe's tea. "Thank you for showing me. I believe I will try tying my cravat that way, too."

"You're welcome, Benji." Marlowe still sounded baffled, but he shrugged away his confusion and picked up the nearest teacup.

When Marlowe drank from the switched cup, his reaction was everything Ben could have hoped for and more. He spat the tea out, right there in the middle of the drawing room.

"Marlowe!" their aunt exclaimed. "What on earth?"

"What the hell? This isn't my cup!" His eyes flicked to the cup in Ben's hand, then up to Ben's face. Something there must have given Ben away, for Marlowe said, "You did that on purpose! You are trying to poison me!"

"What's this about poison?" Aunt Faith demanded. "What are you talking about, Marlowe?"

Ben's smile grew as his cousin realized how he had exposed himself. Marlowe scanned the room. Like Ben, he must have seen how concerned Sir Lewis and Aunt Faith looked.

"Ah ha ha!" Marlowe attempted to laugh it off, but that only made matters worse. Everyone stared at him as he explained, "I must have picked up the wrong cup. This one is far too sweet." He glared at Ben. "It seems to contain more sugar than tea."

"What's wrong with sugar, then?" Sir Lewis spoke in a dangerously soft voice, the one he employed only in serious situations. "A few teaspoons of sugar never hurt anyone. Did it?" He narrowed his eyes.

Before Marlowe could answer, Graves reentered the room and spoke to Sir Lewis. Ben could not catch what the butler whispered, but he heard his father reply, "Yes, send him in. I have some questions."

Then Sir Lewis turned back to Marlowe. "You might be interested in Dr. Gladwell's answers, too, Mr. Millington." He said nothing more, but the cup in Marlowe's hand began to shake.

When Dr. Gladwell entered the room, his eyes immediately alighted on Ben. "Ah, there's young Mr. Radcliffe." He beamed as he said, "Sir, you were right! There *was* arsenic mixed in with the sugar!"

"Arsenic?" In her surprise, Aunt Faith dropped her saucer. The tinkling sound of breaking china filled the whole room. "You mean poison?"

"Oh, God." Marlowe clapped a hand over his mouth. "I must beg to be excused, as I feel very sick."

"You are not going anywhere by yourself," Sir Lewis growled. "Not if I can help it." His eyes flicked towards the open door, where Graves and the footmen stood, not even bothering to hide the fact that they were listening in. "Graves, please send a messenger to the nearest magistrate. We have a crime to report."

Meanwhile, Marlowe tried to make himself vomit, without

success.

Ben sat down, crossed his arms over his chest, and smiled. Eventually, he would inform Marlowe that the sugar in his cup was untainted. For now, he leaned back in his chair and savored his triumph.

$$\sim\!\!\ll\!\!\gg\!\!\sim$$

Chapter Twenty-Four

T HE NEXT TIME Willa called at Marlowe Tower, Ben suggested that they read on the beach, instead of on the cliffs. "I am sure you are better able to tolerate proximity to the ocean now," he said.

Willa wrinkled her nose. She was not at all certain of that! True, she had grown used to the smell of the sea, and she no longer flinched at the cry of the gulls. But thinking about the depths of the ocean, the force of its waves, and the way it swallowed the whole horizon all unsettled her as much as ever.

"You should at least try sitting on the beach," Ben coaxed. "I have a blanket, a hamper full of tea things, and the next volume of *Terror at Carringford Park*. You won't even notice the ocean, because you will have so many other things occupying your attention!"

His tempting wheedle was too much for her powers of resistance. "I suppose it wouldn't hurt. And I *would* like to find out what happens next."

A mischievous grin lurked in both the crinkles around Ben's eyes and the corners of his mouth. "You will hear all sorts of revelations today!" he promised, but he refused to explain further.

Over the last few weeks, Willa and Ben had spent hours reading together on the cliffs above the ocean, but that was very different from sitting on the beach. Every muscle in Willa's body tensed as she descended the stone stairs leading from the cliffs to the beach. Ben preceded Willa down the staircase. That made her feel a little safer—as if the barrier of his body could protect her from the object of her dread.

To her relief, Ben kept them well away from the water. They stuck to the dry area near the cliffs rather than venturing out onto the damp sand. Ben spread a thick rug over the stony ground, then added a softer blanket for good measure.

Willa sat with her back to the water, curling her legs neatly to one side. She could not escape the soft *shhh* of the waves lapping at the shore, but this way she did not have to see the water. Even so, the back of her neck prickled with anxiety. What if an enormous wave reached across the beach and splashed them? What if the tide came in and cut them off from the stairs? What if—?

"You will never believe what happened yesterday." Once Ben had Willa's attention, he told her about the trap he'd set for his cousin. He relayed the story matter-of-factly, without embellishments or exaggerations, but he clearly relished his moment of triumph.

Willa's jaw dropped. For once, she completely forgot about the enormous body of water looming behind her back.

"You mean, I missed all that?" She was one part annoyed she'd missed seeing Ben's moment of triumph and two parts thrilled because Marlowe had confessed.

At least, Marlowe admitted to having known about his sister's plan to poison their grandfather. He insisted, though, that both the idea of poisoning their grandfather and the administration of the arsenic were Almeria's doing. Willa had her doubts about that, though. According to Ben's grandfather, Marlowe stood to inherit much more than Almeria.

"I wish you were there to see the look on his face!" Ben lay back down on the blanket, resting his head on his crossed arms. "Best of all, there were other people on hand to witness his confession. He'll not be able to wiggle out of these charges!" He sounded almost jubilant—but perhaps that was justified, given how much Marlowe bullied him.

Thinking of the possible consequences, Willa frowned. "Is accessory to murder a capital offense?" She did not particularly want Ben's cousins to be executed, but she did not want them running around poisoning sweets, either. She hoped there was a chance of their sentences being commuted to life. Juries often did not like to hang young ladies, which might protect Almeria.

Ben's face fell. "Yes. He and Almeria may very well hang, unless they can convince a jury that the poisoning was an accident of some sort."

Willa snorted. "How could it be an accident when they poisoned three or four different foods?" She ticked the poisonings off on her fingers. "Poisoned peppermints, poisoned fruitcake, poison in the sugar bowl. . . am I missing anything?"

"Those are the only poisoned foods I know about," Ben agreed. "But there could have been earlier poisonings that no one noticed. My grandfather has chronic dyspepsia, after all. It might be easy to mistake arsenic poisoning for one of his regular attacks."

"I suppose it was rather a clever plan on Almeria's part," Willa reluctantly conceded. "But I hope your grandfather recovers. Will he?" She anxiously studied Ben's face. She ought to have asked after Mr. Marlowe's welfare earlier.

"Hard to say," Ben cautioned. "According to Dr. Gladwell, arsenic can sometimes have lasting effects. Grandfather Marlowe is still eating a very limited diet of broth, toast, and tea." He scrunched up his face. "He refuses to take sugar in his tea anymore."

"Who can blame him?" Willa shuddered as she thought about how close Ben himself had come to dying. "I suppose we should be grateful that your cousins were not exactly competent poisoners."

Ben sat up and grinned at her. "Are you sure they were incompetent? Perhaps I am simply a superlative investigator. I should get credit for solving the mystery and forcing a confession. I was quite proud of myself!"

"As you should be." Willa leaned closer to press a kiss against his cheek.

But Ben turned his head so that her lips instead brushed up against his, transforming what she had intended as a chaste sign of affection into a long, slow kiss that deepened, sending heat coursing through Willa's veins. By the time Ben broke the kiss, they were both breathing heavily.

"The poisoning case is not going to delay the wedding, is it?" Ben asked anxiously. "The magistrate originally wanted us to stay in the area for questioning, but when I explained about our plans, he said he could accept a sworn statement from each of us." He frowned. "That is, assuming you still want to get married?"

Willa's heart thudded against her ribs. Was he having doubts? She felt sick as she remembered the condition she'd made when she accepted his proposal. They were both free to back out of the engagement.

"Willa?" Ben prompted. "Are you thinking we ought to end the engagement?"

She licked her lips. "No. No, I am not thinking that. But of course, I entirely understand that you may have been mistaken in your feelings, that—"

He swiftly interrupted her. "I am not mistaken about how much I love you or how much I want to marry you." An anxious smile wavered across his face. "I would marry you tomorrow if I could."

"Oh." Willa closed her eyes as she released a sigh of relief. "Good." She whispered as she added, "Because I love you, too, you know."

For several long minutes, she had no chance to say anything more, because she was too busy kissing Ben.

When they finally drew apart to catch their breaths, Willa grinned her sauciest grin. "I am afraid we cannot marry each other tomorrow," she warned him. "But there should be no delays to the wedding on my side. My usual seamstress is already working on a dress, my uncle has made arrangements for us to use the parish church in Ingleton, and the vicar should be available to perform the ceremony. Unless we ask my uncle Richard to officiate, that is."

As a matter of fact, the question of who should perform the service had become an unexpected point of contention. Since the current Lord Inglewhite had been ordained as a clergyman before he inherited the title, he offered to officiate at the wedding. Willa liked that idea, since she knew Uncle Richard much better than the local vicar. But Willa's mother thought Uncle Richard should give Willa away, since he was her legal guardian.

Before Willa could explain all of that, Ben spoke. "I say, have you noticed that we've been sitting here for nearly half an hour already? Is the ocean still bothering you?"

Willa blinked, surprised. She had been so engrossed in their conversation—and their kisses—that she had ceased to notice the roar of the waves or the pervasive scent of brine. Like the unfathomable mysteries of the ocean, those sensory elements were still present, but they were no longer at the forefront of her mind.

"Maybe I am doing better at ignoring it. At least, when you are here to keep me distracted." A smile broke across her face. She doubted she would ever come to love the seaside, but perhaps she could learn to tolerate it by focusing her attention on something more important.

"Perhaps I had better distract you a little more." Ben drew her into his arms for another long kiss, and Willa found all her senses occupied in the best possible way.

IN THE END, Uncle Rowland solved the question of who should perform the wedding ceremony by arriving unannounced the day before the wedding. He offered to give Willa away, leaving Uncle Richard free to officiate the wedding.

Willa embraced this plan, but she had one concern. "You don't feel slighted, do you?" she whispered to Uncle Richard, as they waited in the vestibule of the church. "I am fond of you, too, you know, and—"

"It is perfectly all right," Uncle Richard whispered back. "I know Rowland is everyone's favorite uncle. He would be *my* favorite too, if I were you. I am not offended."

Willa gasped, because she hadn't meant that at all. When her uncle chuckled, she realized he'd been teasing her.

"I have a daughter of my own to give away someday," Uncle Richard added. "Rowland ought to get his turn, too." He kissed Willa on the cheek and disappeared into the church.

Uncle Rowland was surprisingly nervous about his role. "I am used to being only a spectator at weddings," he reminded Willa. "I suppose I ought to get in practice, in case any of my other nieces have need of me."

He glanced towards the family pew, where both the current Lady Inglewhite and the Dowager Lady sat, accompanied by Phoebe and—rather to Willa's surprise—Rowland's employer. Tall, dark, handsome, and visibly bored, the young Marquis of Reading looked as if he would rather be elsewhere on so fine a morning.

"Why is Lord Reading here?" Willa whispered. "I am flattered that he graced my wedding with his presence, but I hardly know him!" Attending the wedding of his secretary's niece took Lord Reading's responsibility as an employer further than anyone would think necessary.

Uncle Rowland grinned crookedly. "Yes, but if he hadn't come along, he and I would be separated for days. I like to think that after all these years, he cannot get by without me," he joked. "In any case, between Lord Francis's children and Ivy's brood, Reading has even more nieces, nephews, and young cousins in Ingleton than I do. You might not be able to tell by looking at him, but he is very fond of all the children in the family."

"I suppose that makes sense." There certainly *were* a lot of children gathered in the church today. Willa recognized Uncle Richard's two eldest (the baby had stayed in the nursery), but she did not know who all the others were.

"Besides," Rowland added, "Reading wanted an excuse to get out of the city. No one wants to be in London in July."

That was indisputable. It was one of the reasons why Willa had never even considered holding her wedding at St. George's, the preferred location for *ton* weddings. Neither Willa nor Ben thought a fashionable wedding was worth suffering the stifling heat and foul odors of London in the summer.

Uncle Richard cleared his throat and said "Dearly Beloved" in a voice loud enough to carry all the way up to the church's open rafters. Everyone's attention shifted to the front of the church.

As the service began, Willa had eyes for no one but Ben, who seemed far more nervous than she was. In fact, he fumbled the ring, but Willa caught it before it could hit the floor. Ben's ears turned bright red, but the ceremony continued without further incident.

The moment Ben and Will stepped out of the church, wedding bells rang a celebratory peal. People from the castle and the village swarmed around the bride and groom, shouting, laughing, wishing them well, and generally making merry.

Ben, who did not like crowds or loud noises, cringed. Willa patted his hand reassuringly as she guided them out of the crowd. When they reached the long gravel carriageway back up the hill to the castle, they finally had a little space to themselves.

"We are married!" Willa whispered to her new husband. "For richer or poorer, in sickness or health." Those words lingered in her mind even after the final blessing.

"I think you mean, in the depths of the ocean or the darkness of space," Ben quipped. "I still think we ought to have gone to the Orkney Islands for our honeymoon."

Willa glared at him. "There will be no sea voyages of any

kind on our honeymoon," she insisted. They had agreed to spend the first weeks of their married life in the Lake District, well away from the seashore.

But, as it turned out, their honeymoon did include a glance into the heights of the heavens. Three days after their wedding, Willa and Ben carried a pair of thick blankets from their rented cottage out into an empty pasture. They spread one blanket on the ground so they could lie back and look up at the stars and tucked the other one around them to keep warm. Even in July, the night breeze carried a chill.

Out here, far from the nearest neighbors, there were more stars in the sky than Willa could ever remember seeing. The cloudy band of the Milky Way spread across the sky.

As she stared up into the mysterious darkness, earth and its inhabitants seemed miniscule by contrast. All that held her in place was the invisible hand of gravity. For a dizzying moment, Willa felt as if she might fall off into the depths of space.

But only for a moment. She reached for Ben's hand and twined her fingers with his. "I see why you said that the immensity of the night sky frightened you." She hesitated for a moment before asking, "Does it frighten you now?"

"Hmm." He squeezed her hand more tightly. "It might frighten me if you were not here. But you anchor me to the ground, and I know I will not fall."

The unexpected sweetness of that sentiment put a lump in Willa's throat. "I suppose enormous things like that—high mountains, deep waters, and so on—frighten us because they are awesome in the literal sense. They inspire awe, and awe is only hair's breadth away from fear."

"It works the other way around, too, you know," Ben pointed out. "Fear is related to awe, but so is reverence. That is what the sublime is all about, isn't it? Reverence and fear bound together in the face of power and majesty."

He turned to press his lips against her cheek. "Maybe someday you will look at the ocean with reverence, too."

Willa squeezed his hand as she imagined that. In this romantic moment, all things seemed possible. She could at least turn her mind away from the ocean's dreadful vastness to subjects both more pleasant and closer to the hand.

"Maybe my fears will not matter so much, as long as I am moored in your love." She turned away from the distant stars to the husband by her side, and they kissed beneath the starry sky.

The End

Author's Note

Like many of the fictional characters I write, Benjamin Radcliffe is coded as autistic. The neurological differences that we call autism existed in his time, though the concept of autism as a specific neurotype or disorder did not.

The word "phobia," used to describe an "irrational" or "extreme" fear, has been in use since the late 1700s. In 1822, however, Wilhelmina Selwyn's fear of the ocean had not yet been given the name "thalassophobia." Today, specific phobias such as fear of heights or fear of the ocean are considered anxiety disorders.

In writing both characters, I have drawn from both my own experience and from research into these conditions.

Acknowledgments

The Case at Castle Rock Cove concludes the Beau Monde Secrets quartet. It has been a joy to see these books enter the world, but it has taken a lot of work to get here! Many people have helped along the way. At Dragonblade Publishing, I am particularly grateful for Ariele Riviere's editing, which helped me deepen conflict and narrative tension, and for Dar Albert, who designed gorgeous covers for each of the books.

I also want to thank the many beta readers and sensitivity readers who helped make this series stronger. For example, Petra P. and Ally both provided beta readings that helped me strengthen the romance arc in *Secrets at Selwyn Castle*. Brooke gave advice on *The Case at Castle Rock Cove* that similarly helped me deepen the romance between Ben and Willa.

If you've read the whole series, you may have noticed that many of the Beau Monde Secrets books feature disabled or neurodivergent lead characters. Writing such characters is daunting even when I share their disabilities and neurotypes! Thankfully, I've had many folks to help me along the way. When I struggled with writing a well-rounded, authentically depicted autistic female lead in *Discovery at Dogwood* Cottage, Petra P. and Leslie S. helped me see ways Arabella Canning could be fleshed out into a more rounded character. Brooke provided great disability-focused readings of *The Incident at Ingleton* and *The Case at Castle Rock Cove*. I am also grateful for the support of the authors in my Disabled Romance Writers chat. Thank you all for being there to listen to complaints, suggest resources, and help me brainstorm. All mistakes are my own.

Finally, I am grateful for all my readers. I hope you've enjoyed this series!

About the Author

Anne Rollins is the pen name of an English professor who lives in Northern California with her family, too many cats, and an enormous collection of books. She has spent untold hours of her life rereading Georgette Heyer novels, and hopes that someday people will compulsively reread her novels, too!

Join me at the following:
annerollins.com
facebook.com/profile.php?id=100094523334798
instagram.com/annerollins23
threads.net/@annerollins23

www.ingramcontent.com/pod-product-compliance
Lightning Source LLC
Chambersburg PA
CBHW060417310726
48976CB00003B/1084